"Joe," Sally cooed.
"Welcome to *Kiss the Bride!*"

The reality TV hostess gestured to Casey. "The show where you marry the woman of your dreams. Doesn't she look gorgeous?"

Joe opened his mouth, but it took him a couple of tries to get any words out. "She does," he managed to say at last.

Relief washed over Casey, restoring her heart to its normal rhythm. *It's going to be all right.*

"Joe, this is your big moment," Sally said. "All you have to do is pop the question and you can marry Casey right here." She beamed encouragement.

Joe hesitated. Casey gave him what she intended to be a loving smile, although she was afraid it might have emerged as pleading. Still he hesitated.

"Joe, aren't you going to ask Casey to marry you?" Sally sounded like a mother addressing a recalcitrant child.

Joe spoke, loud and clear this time. "N... ...t."

Dear Reader,

Do you find it difficult to say no when someone asks you to help out? Me, too! Of course, helping out is always a wonderful thing to do…but sometimes you can't help feeling as if you have Pushover tattooed on your forehead.

In *Married by Mistake,* Casey Greene decides she's finished with being a pushover. Unfortunately, her fight for the no-strings love she's always wanted goes disastrously wrong; she ends up accidentally married to Adam Carmichael. Adam might be Memphis's most eligible bachelor, but he never does anything he doesn't want to. Yet when a reformed pushover and a man of granite go head-to-head, anything can happen!

I hope you enjoy Adam and Casey's story. Please e-mail me at abby@abbygaines.com and let me know what you think.

If you're like me, when you get to the end of a book, you wish there was just a little more to read about those characters you've grown attached to. Well, with this book, there is! If you'd like to see how the romance of minor characters Sam and Eloise came to its happy ending—and how Casey and Adam renewed their wedding vows—visit the For Readers page at www.abbygaines.com to read a couple of special extra scenes.

Abby Gaines

MARRIED BY MISTAKE
Abby Gaines

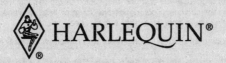

TORONTO • NEW YORK • LONDON
AMSTERDAM • PARIS • SYDNEY • HAMBURG
STOCKHOLM • ATHENS • TOKYO • MILAN • MADRID
PRAGUE • WARSAW • BUDAPEST • AUCKLAND

ISBN-13: 978-0-373-71414-8
ISBN-10:   0-373-71414-9

MARRIED BY MISTAKE

ABOUT THE AUTHOR

Abby Gaines wrote for five years before she sold her first novel to Harlequin Superromance (*Whose Lie Is It Anyway?* January 2007). Fortunately, she got used to the barrage of rejection letters—though she never quite embraced them in the way some people recommend—and didn't lose heart. During those years she worked as a business journalist and also as editor of a speedway magazine. So it's no wonder her next book will be published as part of the Harlequin NASCAR series (*Back on Track,* May 2007).

Abby lives with her husband and children in an olive grove. She says olive trees are perfect to inspire the funny, tender romances she loves to write.

For Nigel, who mostly succeeds in being an immovable object, but when it really matters, is putty in my hands....

CHAPTER ONE

THE BRIDE WORE A long white dress and a look of utter despair.

Adam Carmichael saw her through the glass wall of the Memphis Channel Eight boardroom, scurrying down the corridor as fast as the full skirt of her dress would allow, flicking furtive glances over her shoulder.

Damn, a runaway bride. Could this day get any worse?

He stepped out of the boardroom, and she saved him the effort of stopping her when she cannoned into him, preoccupied by one of those over-the-shoulder checks. Soft yet firm breasts pressed hard against Adam's chest; honey-gold hair tickled his chin.

He steadied her with his hands on her upper arms. And saw tears welling in her eyes. Instantly he released her, took a step back.

She brushed at the tears with short, impatient movements. "I'm sorry, I didn't mean to…" She looked behind her again and said distractedly,

"Anyway, it was nice meeting you, but I really must…"

She gathered up her skirt, ready to run, giving Adam a glimpse of slim ankles above a pair of silk shoes.

Overhead, the PA system crackled to life, and Adam recognized the voice of Channel Eight's senior producer, unusually agitated. "Would Casey Greene please return to makeup immediately. Casey Greene to makeup." There was a pause, then the producer said, "Now!" more ferociously than Adam had ever heard her speak before.

There was no mistaking the whimper from the runaway bride, nor the flare of panic in her eyes, which were the gray-green of the Mississippi when a storm was brewing.

Adam clamped a hand over her forearm. "Sounds like they're looking for you."

"I can't go back." She tried to tug her arm free.

Fleetingly, he considered letting her go. But much as he hated this wedding show, he wasn't about to sabotage it.

They were due to go live in an hour, so it was a safe bet people would be scouring the building for the missing bride. In her panic to get away, she'd obviously taken the elevator up instead of down. It might take awhile for the search party to reach the top-floor boardroom, but they'd get here in the end.

"You can't leave like this," he said. "You look

terrible." Oops, that wasn't the most tactful thing to say to a bride. "I mean, you look great…fantastic." He ran a quick eye over her to check if he'd made a fair assessment. She was a little on the short side, around five-four in her shoes, he estimated, but the dress hugged some very attractive curves.

He pushed open the door to the boardroom. "Why don't you take a minute to pull yourself together?" He gave her no chance to refuse, shepherding her in, then steering her to one of the black leather couches arranged along the far wall. He turned a chair from the boardroom table around to face her, and sat down. "I assume you're Casey Greene?"

She nodded. Someone walked past the boardroom, and she shrank down in the couch.

"It's only my secretary," he assured her. But she looked jittery, as if she might spring up at any moment. Adam estimated it had been a minute since that call over the PA, probably several minutes since she'd left her minders. Where *were* those guys? He said chattily, "So you're a guest on *Kiss the Bride?*"

"I was."

Uh-oh. This was just what he needed, after he'd worked through the night to get this show into some semblance of order, tying up the loose ends his cousin Henry, the show's creator, had overlooked. Except Adam hadn't had time to check if Henry had lined up a replacement bridal couple in case someone pulled out. He'd bet money the answer was no.

Any minute now, representatives of the show's sponsor, New Visage Cosmetics, would arrive at the studio to see the debut of "their" show. New Visage was in a different league from Channel Eight's other sponsors; having them on board would bring the station to the attention of the major players. Adam couldn't afford for anything to go wrong.

He wanted to haul this woman back to the production suite—anyone dumb enough to sign up for a surprise wedding show deserved whatever she got. "It's understandable you have cold feet. Just remember, this is the happiest day of your life."

He couldn't have sounded very convincing, for she shot him an unbridelike glare.

"Oh, sure," she said. "I dupe my fiancé into coming to the TV studio, and he won't find out until we're on air that he's here to get married. Happy days."

Adam should never have left Henry in charge while he was in New York. His cousin must have had this crazy idea in mind for months, to have set the show up in just four weeks. Adam had come home two days ago to find the station abuzz with excitement about *Kiss the Bride.*

He could have canned it. But then the family stockholders would accuse him of being high-handed again. Better to let tonight run its course, then convince New Visage to put their money into a higher quality program.

The muted sound of the PA system drifted in from the corridor. "Paging Casey Greene. If anyone has seen Casey Greene could they please notify Production immediately."

Adam eyed the telephone on the boardroom table.

Casey stiffened. "You wouldn't."

He would, if he didn't think it would scare her into resuming her escape. He had an hour of live TV to fill, the viewers had been promised a wedding show and that's what they would get. A show delivered to the highest possible standard. Which meant no empty seats on the set. "How about we let the crew know you're okay?"

Her eyes narrowed. "Who *are* you?"

"Adam Carmichael." There was no flash of recognition—he had to assume she didn't read those magazines that voted him Memphis's Most Eligible Bachelor. "I run this place."

"So you can get me out of here? Off the show?" She stood in a flurry of excitement, a hopeful smile curving her mouth, crinkling the corners of those gray-green eyes, hinting at a dimple in her right cheek.

"Why don't you tell me," he hedged, "exactly what the problem is?"

Her smile faded and she sat down again. "You're not going to help, are you? Don't worry, I'll figure it out myself."

Adam hadn't missed the vulnerability that shadowed her eyes.

The vulnerability that made her not his type.

"Have you changed your mind about the wedding?" Maybe he could find someone—a woman, someone happily married, anyone but him—to talk her around.

"Not exactly. I'm desperate, or I wouldn't have resorted to coming on *Kiss the Bride.*"

She didn't look desperate. With her eyes still bright with moisture and her cheeks flushed at the personal nature of the conversation, she looked more than ordinarily attractive, like the kind of woman who would have potential bridegrooms lining up on her doorstep.

"Is your fiancé giving you trouble?"

Casey shook her head. "Joe is pretty well perfect. Kind, good-looking, honest—fun to be with."

"He sounds great," Adam said heartily. "How about we get you to the studio so you can marry him?"

Okay, so that wasn't subtle. She fixed him with a stung, accusatory expression. "But what about love?"

Adam felt the kick of a headache at his left temple. He looked through the glass, out into the empty corridor. How the hell could the production team be doing such a bad job of finding this woman? "I don't know," he said cautiously. "What *about* love?"

Casey eased back into the cushions, as if he'd hit on her favorite subject. "I love Joe, and he loves me." She spread her hands, palms up. "We wouldn't have got engaged otherwise, would we?"

"I suppose not," Adam said.

"But sometimes, people love you for what you can do for them, as much as for who you are, and it's hard to tell the difference. I always wanted a husband who'd adore me just for myself, and someone I adored back. Real love, no strings attached." Her finger traced the piping that edged one of the cushions. "If I'm honest, that's not what Joe and I have."

Adam groaned. Poor Joe, expected to "adore" this woman for the rest of her days, when, if he was anything like most guys, all he wanted was a quiet life.

Her eyes sparked in annoyance. "Don't you think people should hold out for their dreams?"

"I think people should figure out what they *want,* then go for it," Adam said. "But…a guy who adores you? No strings?" He shook his head. "Those are teenage daydreams."

She thought that over. "You mean, you used to dream of marrying a woman who adored you, but you grew out of it?"

Adam cast another longing glance at the phone. "The last thing a teenage boy wants is to be adored by some woman for the rest of his life." *Some of us never grow out of that.* "Boys dream about NASCAR racing."

"Did you?"

If sharing that misguided ambition would get her back on the show, Adam would do it. He nodded. "Believe me, I never regretted joining the family business instead."

Even if he had run off to Charlotte, the racing capital, he'd probably still be on the receiving end of constant demands from his grasping relatives.

"Are you married?"

Did he *look* like a sucker for punishment?

She rushed on without waiting for him to reply, as if it was a relief to be revealing her doubts. At least someone was enjoying this. "Joe and I started dating in high school. We drifted into our engagement at graduation—that was seven years ago. We said we'd wait until we could afford to buy a house before we got married."

"Good idea," Adam said. He inched his hand toward the phone.

"Every time we set a wedding date, something happens to change our plans," she said. "But now I need to hurry things up. Now, I *have* to get married."

A shock of…surprise surged through Adam, and he forgot about the phone. He stole another quick look at Casey's figure, to see if he'd missed any suspicious bulges. No sign of a baby—but pregnancy would explain her emotional state.

She looked as if she was about to break down again. Adam, inured to tears through years of dealing with weepy female relatives, planned to wait her out. But something about the way Casey's eyes shimmered, then widened as if to say she wasn't about to cry, no, not at all, got to him. He whipped his handkerchief out of his pocket and offered it to her.

She took it without a word. He read the Emergency Fire Instructions pinned to the wall while he tried to ignore the way her snuffling did funny things to his insides. Eventually he gave up, and glanced sideways long enough to find and pat the creamy shoulder nearest him. At his touch, Casey straightened, drew on some inner reserve to blink the tears away, and met Adam's gaze full on.

"I'm sorry." She blew her nose one last time.

"Why don't you tell me more about Joe?" Dwelling on her husband-to-be's good points might cheer her up.

"He's very nice. We have a lot in common," she said. "He's about to join the navy, which means he'll be away a lot, but I can handle that."

For all Casey's dreams of being adored, Adam would bet the marriage she had lined up with Joe would be a lot happier than one based on some infatuation.

"Unless," Casey said, "I pull out now, and wait for a man who adores me."

He wished she wouldn't keep saying that. She had stars in her eyes when she talked about love and adoring.

Besides, if Casey was pregnant, she should

marry the father of her child. The pretty-well-perfect father of her child.

"You could wait a long time for a man who adores you," Adam said, and was annoyed to find he felt like a heel, telling her to abandon her dreams. More forcefully, he added, "You might never find one. Marry Joe and be happy with what you've got."

"Casey!" A voice from the doorway startled them. Adam recognized one of the production assistants. *About time.* Casey leaped to her feet.

"There you are." The woman's voice was overly bright. She flashed Adam a look of sympathetic exasperation. "They're waiting for you in makeup. We need to hurry."

Casey hesitated. She swallowed, then turned to Adam. "You're right, I'm sure it'll be fine." Her voice held the faintest question, so Adam nodded reassuringly. She smiled, a proper smile this time, which made her eyes glow more green than gray. "It was nice talking to you."

"You, too. And—" he might as well admit he knew what she'd been alluding to "—good luck with the baby."

Her eyes widened. He saw confusion, the dawn of understanding, then amusement chasing through them. She laughed out loud. "I'm not pregnant."

"So why did you say you have to get married?"

She beamed, still amused. "It's complicated.

Family stuff." She stuck out a hand and said, "Bye, Adam."

"Goodbye, Casey. And good luck." Whether it was because he knew what desperate measures family could drive a person to, or because he felt unaccountably relieved she wasn't pregnant, or just because she was dressed in such formal, elaborate style, Adam did the weirdest thing. Instead of shaking her hand, he lifted it to his mouth, pressed a kiss to the back of her fingers.

And found himself sorely tempted to kiss Casey Greene all the way up her arm and keep right on going.

CASEY HAD CONVINCED herself she had her nerves under control. She'd gotten over that crazy bout of crying in front of a complete stranger. She'd gone through makeup, final adjustments to her hair and the fitting of her veil, ninety-five percent certain that following her dream justified this extreme step.

Now, a renewed surge of misgiving tightened her grip on the seat of the high stool center stage in the baking-hot television studio. The show hadn't started; a buzz of conversation drifted from the studio audience toward the stage.

"Remind me why I'm doing this," she muttered to the bride on her right, her best friend, Brodie-Ann Evans. Beyond Brodie-Ann, the third bride overheard the question and tittered. She'd introduced herself as Trisha from Truberg and, in her wedding dress, was alarmingly reminiscent of a giggling meringue.

"Two words," Brodie-Ann said. "Push. Over."

Oh, yeah. I am not a pushover. Not anymore. Casey recalled the way Joe kept postponing the date for their wedding, and how their plans to move out of Parkvale kept getting put on hold. Then she summoned to mind the letter she'd received last month from her sister, Karen. A letter that gave Casey the urge to get as far away as possible from their hometown.

It was time her life started happening, and tonight was the night.

"Thanks, hon," she breathed to Brodie-Ann.

Signing up for the pilot episode of *Kiss the Bride* had been Brodie-Ann's idea—but Casey had instantly recognized its genius. If her best friend could marry the man she loved after dating him just six months, then Casey would darn well marry Joe.

Which was how she'd ended up here, dressed in a silk-and-lace concoction she could never have afforded in real life.

The floor director, who'd introduced himself earlier, stepped up on to the stage in front of Casey. "Two minutes, ladies, so get ready to smile. And remember, don't look at the cameras while you're being interviewed."

Instinctively, Casey's gaze darted to the nearest camera, which appeared to be pointed right at her. The director tsked. "Keep your eyes on Sally, the camera will find you." He paused, pressed his headphones against one ear as he listened, then smiled at the brides. "I'm happy to report that your men are ready and waiting in the green room. No cold feet." He nodded brisk reassurance, then hurried to talk to Sally.

Casey wasn't surprised to hear the men weren't worried.

She'd told Joe they were competing on a game show and were likely to win a lot of money. They'd driven three hours to Memphis this morning. Brodie-Ann's boyfriend, Steve, along with a third unsuspecting man had been taken out for lunch by Channel Eight staff and given bogus details as to what the show was about. They doubtless assumed their female partners were getting the same treatment.

How could it have occurred to Joe that Casey would be selecting a wedding dress, having a makeover and planning on marrying him in front of millions of viewers?

She shuddered. Thank goodness it was only a local show. No one outside of Tennessee would see what she'd had to go through to get married.

"I'm not conning Joe into marrying me," she told Brodie-Ann. "I'm just bringing the date forward a bit."

"You told me that already. Twelve times."

Casey closed her eyes and prayed she wasn't crazy.

What *was* crazy was that her fingers should still be tingling from the kiss of a stranger. Worse, as she tried to conjure up Joe's face, that same stranger's image kept intruding.

Adam Carmichael was the kind of guy any woman would think about, she consoled herself. Those broad shoulders, those strong hands that had steadied her… At first, Casey had thought his eyes an arctic blue, but when he kissed her, they'd glinted a warmer azure color. Most of the time he'd looked tense, with a furrow in his brow that told her the tension might be habitual.

When Casey opened her eyes, Adam stood in her line of vision, next to the camera she wasn't supposed to be looking at. He was looking right at her, frowning again. She couldn't see that furrow, but she knew it would be there. She guessed he might be worrying about her, and her delusions of romance.

She mustered a reassuring smile—*I'm not going to fall apart*—and waggled her fingers at him. He waved back, but it was a brief, tense movement.

A production assistant clipped a microphone to her dress, obscuring Casey's view of Adam. When the assistant stepped aside, he was gone. A peculiar loneliness made her chest ache.

Then someone was counting down. Sally Summers, the show's host, looked in the mirror one last time and…they were on air. It took all Casey's willpower not to flee the set as Sally began her introduction. The words passed Casey by, but she was jerked back to reality when Sally came over to interview Trisha from Truberg.

"Trisha, how long have you and Martin been dating?"

Five years, Trisha told Sally. They'd been engaged for three, and their families still couldn't agree on a wedding date.

After the interview, a drumroll rounded to a crescendo, then Sally called Martin Blake to the set. He emerged from backstage to the strains of "Here Comes the Bride," and the audience applauded on cue. Martin did a double take, but to Casey's relief—*maybe this won't be so bad*—he got over his initial shock.

Sally explained he could marry Trisha right now. The deputy clerk of Shelby County Court would issue a marriage license and a minister would perform the ceremony. Then Martin and Trisha would head off on a luxury honeymoon.

Martin scratched his head. "Now? Tonight?"

Sally repeated the offer, this time stressing that the honeymoon was all-expenses-paid.

"Just think, baby," Trisha coaxed him, "no more arguing with your mom about the wedding." She giggled as she darted a look at the camera. "Oops, sorry, Mrs. Blake."

Maybe that was the clincher, because Martin said, "You're right, hon, let's do it." Trisha squealed with delight. The marriage license was completed during the commercial break, and when they were back on air, the minister stepped up. Five minutes later, Trisha had her wish.

"That went okay," Casey murmured, as the audience clapped. Brodie-Ann didn't reply. She appeared frozen in her seat, as if she'd only just realized what tonight was all about.

After the next commercial break, Sally introduced Brodie-Ann to the audience and invited her to tell everyone about Steve.

"He's the most wonderful guy I ever met," she said, the quaver in her voice barely discernible. "We haven't been together long, but I adore everything about him. I know he's the one."

The audience oohed appreciatively.

Casey felt a twinge of envy. She couldn't remember ever loving Joe like that.

Then it was Steve's turn to come on stage. He was a smart guy; it took him only half a second to realize what "Here Comes the Bride" and Brodie-Ann in a long white dress meant. A huge grin split his face. He stepped right up to her, went down on one knee and said, "Sweetheart, will you marry me?"

The crowd went wild—and they did again when, at the end of the brief ceremony, Steve and Brodie-

Ann shared a kiss that raised the temperature in the studio by several degrees. Then the new Mr. and Mrs. Pemberton joined Trisha and her husband on the studio couch.

"TELL ME THIS ISN'T CRAP," Adam demanded of his good friend Dave Dubois, who was standing next to him at the back of the control room. As a freelance programming consultant, Dave occasionally worked with Channel Eight. He hadn't been involved with this show. But he was keen to see it. In front of them, the show's director focused intently on a wide, multiwindow screen. The footage currently being broadcast played out in the large center window. Smaller windows around it displayed feeds from the other cameras. Adam could see Casey, the last bride, in one of those windows.

"It sure isn't your normal kind of show." Dave's response lacked the contempt Adam would have welcomed.

"It's no one's normal kind of show. It's my cousin Henry's kind of show."

The director said into his headset, "Ready, two, with a close-up on bride three. Standby mics and cue." Camera two obediently zoomed in on Casey, ready for her to take center screen. Her jaw appeared to be clenched so tightly she risked breaking a tooth.

"Look." Dave pointed to the image feed from camera three. The studio audience was apparently enthralled by the whole tacky proceedings. To Adam's irritation, his friend evaded the opportunity to savage Henry, settling for an ambiguous, "You're still the boss around here, right?"

"If you mean does my charming family still see me as the bad guy, you bet. If you mean does fear of me stop Henry creating idiotic new shows while I'm out of town…"

"Hmm," Dave said. "Any progress on the legal front?"

Just what Adam wanted to think about right now. He sent his friend a withering look.

Dave said hastily, "Y'know, this show's not bad. And the reality market is still booming, no matter what the doomsayers predict."

If he'd intended to distract Adam from thoughts of the lawsuit that Henry and his mother had insti-gated against Adam, he'd picked the wrong topic. Adam fixed him with a black look.

"Okay, so it's not the last word in good taste," Dave admitted. "But it's got pretty women—that third bride is a real babe. It's got romance and happy endings. Though I do think something's missing."

"A dancing girl bearing Henry's head on a platter?"

Dave gave the suggestion due consideration. "You're on the right track. The whole thing needs more tension. More drama."

ANOTHER COMMERCIAL BREAK, then they were back on air. Casey licked her dry lips, feeling very alone at center stage. She looked around for Adam, but couldn't find him.

"Folks, this is Casey Greene. She's come all the way from Parkvale for today's show," Sally announced.

The crowd cheered, expecting great things from another Parkvale girl.

"Casey is twenty-five. She's a journalist and a psychology student, and she wants to be a novelist," Sally continued. "What do you want to write, Casey?"

"Books," she answered numbly.

"And your fiancé is Joe Elliott," Sally added brightly. "Tell us about you and Joe."

"We met in high school, and we got engaged at graduation." If she'd been any more wooden, they'd call her Pinocchio. *Relax*. Casey exhaled slowly through her nose.

"How's that, folks? High school sweethearts!" Sally tried to rally some enthusiasm from the crowd, but their applause was muted. They must have sensed this wasn't the love story of the decade. "Casey, tell us what you love about Joe."

Casey's mind went blank. "Uh, he's, uh…"

Sally's smile froze.

"He's so honest," Casey said at last. "So handsome." Silence. For Pete's sake, they wanted more?

"I've known him forever. And...I can't imagine being with anyone else."

At least she couldn't until about an hour ago, when a stranger had left the imprint of his lips on her hand. She glanced quickly down at her fingers—of course there was no sign of Adam's kiss. "I really want to get married," she said, and added, with an emphasis that was too loud and too late, "to Joe."

At last the interview was over. The strains of "Here Comes the Bride" filled the studio. Across the stage, Joe appeared. He stopped dead, looked around, saw the other two couples on the couch, heard the audience chanting, "Joe, Joe, Joe," and, finally, looked at Casey. A dragging inevitability slowed his progress across the stage.

"Joe," Sally cooed. "Welcome to *Kiss the Bride,* the show where you marry the woman of your dreams." She gestured to Casey. "Doesn't she look gorgeous?"

Joe opened his mouth, but it took him a couple of tries to get any words out. "She does," he managed to answer at last.

Relief washed over Casey, restoring her heart to its normal rhythm. *It's going to be all right.*

"Joe, this is your big moment," Sally said. "All you have to do is pop the question, and you can marry Casey right here." Her brilliant smile encouraged him.

Joe hesitated. Casey gave him what she intended

to be a loving smile, though she feared it might have emerged as pleading. Still he hesitated.

"Joe, aren't you going to ask Casey to marry you?" Sally sounded like a mother addressing a recalcitrant child.

Joe spoke, loud and clear this time.

"No, I'm not."

CHAPTER TWO

"YES!" DAVE DUBOIS PUNCHED the air with his fist. "You did it, buddy. This is much better than Henry's head on a plate."

Adam cursed as the center screen flipped from one camera feed to the next as the director searched for something other than frozen expressions and hanging jaws. So much for convincing New Visage Cosmetics that Channel Eight could mount a professional, sophisticated production.

With Dave on his heels, he rushed out of the control room and into the studio, where stunned silence had given way to a hubbub of excited chatter.

On the set, Sally Summers's famous smile had evaporated. Joe stepped toward Casey, and the microphone clipped to his shirt picked up what he said, despite his low voice.

"I'm sorry, Casey, but I don't want to marry you— I don't love you that way anymore. I didn't want to hurt your feelings…." He stopped, perhaps aware his words were being broadcast around Tennessee.

Make that the entire U.S.A.

As Adam headed to the front of the studio he noticed Channel Eight's PR manager had pulled out her cell phone and was talking in urgent tones. She'd be instructing her assistants to get this story on the late news. By tomorrow, she'd have sold the program nationwide. Casey's disaster was great TV.

Joe said again, "I'm sorry." Then he turned and—as if he hadn't done enough damage—all but ran offstage. Sally patted Casey's hand in what might have been intended as a gesture of comfort, but looked perfunctory.

Adam headed for his cousin Henry, next to camera three. To reach him, he had to pass the New Visage executives, huddled in anxious consultation in their front-row seats.

"Adam." Henry's round face was flushed with panic. He grabbed Adam's arm. "I had no idea this would happen, I swear."

Damn, that meant there was no contingency plan.

Henry jerked his head toward the stage. "Do you think she's going to faint?"

Adam looked up at Casey, swaying on her stool, blinking rapidly.

Behind him, the chatter of the studio audience swelled to an unruly level. He shut out the sound, focused on what needed to be done. *One, restore order to the studio. Two, salvage the show so New*

Visage doesn't pull the plug. Three, get Casey out of here before she decides to sue Carmichael Broadcasting for public humiliation.

"Tell the crew to follow my lead on this," he told Henry. His cousin began issuing hurried instructions to the floor director, who was in radio contact with the director in the control room. To Dave, Adam said, "How good an actor are you?"

"I played a tree in *The Wizard of Oz* in fifth grade."

"I hope you were a damn good one," Adam said. "Wait here until I tell you to come up on stage. Then do as I say."

The security people let Adam through and he stepped up onto the stage. Sally became aware of his presence. She turned and took a few hesitant steps in his direction.

"Mr. Carmichael," she said, then remembered to flash her dazzling smile. "Welcome to *Kiss the Bride,* the show where—"

He stalked up to her and motioned to her to mute her mic. When he was sure no one would hear him, he said, "We need to fix this—*now.*"

"How do you propose we do that?" she hissed.

"That bride—" he nodded toward Casey "—is going to have a wedding." He added grimly, "Even if I have to marry her myself."

"You can't do—"

"You're going to help."

Sally flicked a yearning glance over his shoulder

at her teleprompter. When no script appeared, she started to shake her head.

"Right now, Sally." Adam dropped his voice to a menacing murmur. "Your contract negotiations are due at the end of the quarter."

Sally Summers was nothing if not pragmatic. Adam could almost see the dollar signs in her eyes as she turned to the audience wearing a wide smile that only the two of them knew was false. She switched her mic back on and stepped forward.

"Well, folks, the course of true love never runs smooth, and who knows that better than Casey? But tonight, one man's loss might be another man's gain. It turns out Casey has another admirer here in the studio, a man waiting in the wings—literally— for his chance at love."

Adam winced at the stream of clichés. But Sally was headed in the right direction, however painful the route she took to get there.

"Folks—" she was warming to her task and by now had some real enthusiasm in her voice "—meet Adam Carmichael, Memphis's most eligible bachelor. And, if she'll have him, Casey Greene's bridegroom!"

The audience broke into a cheer, which Adam suspected was more out of confusion than celebration. He strode over to where Casey clung dazedly to her stool, and took both her hands in his. She clutched them as if he'd thrown her a lifeline.

"Casey—" he spoke loudly so his words would carry to the audience without a mic "—will you marry me?"

He heard a shriek from someone in the crowd. Casey stared at him. He leaned forward, and his lips skimmed the soft skin of her cheek as he whispered in her ear, "We're going to fake a wedding."

He stepped back and said again, for the benefit of the crowd, "Casey, will you marry me? Please?"

He wondered if she'd understood, she sat there, unresponsive, for so long. Then she expelled a slow breath and smiled radiantly, her gray-green eyes full of trust. "Yes, Adam, I will."

For a second, he felt a tightness in his chest, as if he'd just seriously proposed marriage to the woman he loved. Whatever that might feel like. A din exploded around them, the audience cheering, Sally yelling to make herself heard. Someone called for a commercial break.

Five minutes later, the clerk had issued a marriage license. Under Tennessee law there was no waiting period, no blood test. Adam announced he would use his own marriage celebrant, and beckoned to Dave. His friend looked around, then twigged that Adam meant him. He bounded forward, and by the time he reached the set his face was a study in solemnity. If you discounted the gleam in his eyes.

Dave patted his pockets, then turned to the

ousted minister. "I seem to have forgotten my vows. Could I borrow yours?"

Just as they went back on air he clipped on a microphone. He began laboring through the "wedding."

"Adam James Carmichael, do you take—" He slanted Casey a questioning look.

"Casey Eleanor Greene," she supplied.

"Casey Eleanor Greene to be your wife? To have and to hold, for—"

"I do," Adam said.

"Right." Dave moved down the page. "Casey Eleanor Greene, do you—"

"I do," Casey said.

"—take Adam James Carmichael to be your husband?"

"She said she does," Adam snapped.

At the same moment, Casey repeated desperately, "I do!"

Dave got the message and started to wrap things up. "Then, uh—" he lost his place and improvised "—it's a deal. You're married, husband and wife. You may—"

"Kiss the bride!" the audience yelled on cue.

Why not? They'd gone through all the other motions of a wedding. Adam turned to Casey and found she'd lifted her face expectantly.

One kiss and this nightmare would be over, Casey told herself. She could escape the scene of her utter humiliation, and barricade herself in the house in Parkvale for the next hundred years.

Going after your dreams was vastly overrated.

She leaned toward Adam, went up on tiptoe to make it easier for him to seal this sham. *Just kiss the guy and we can all go home.*

She wasn't prepared for the same current of electricity that had left her fingers tingling earlier to multiply tenfold as their mouths met.

Shaken, she grasped his upper arms to steady herself, and encountered the steel of masculine strength through the fine wool of his jacket. His hands went to her waist and he pulled her closer. The shock of awareness that somewhere deep within her a flame of desire had been kindled snapped Casey's eyes open. She met Adam's gaze full on, saw mirrored in it her own realization that this was about to get embarrassing. Even more embarrassing.

Slowly, he pulled back.

The audience hooted in appreciation. Casey blushed.

"Folks, none of us expected this when we came on stage an hour ago, but there you have it. Casey Greene married Adam Carmichael, right here on *Kiss the Bride.*" Sally ad-libbed with ease, now that time was up. "These three lovely couples will head off on their honeymoons, courtesy of Channel Eight. Don't miss next week's show—anything can happen on *Kiss the Bride!*"

Casey and Adam didn't wait around for the inevitable interrogation. By unspoken agreement, they headed offstage and back to the boardroom where they'd met—could it really have been just two hours ago?

Casey sank onto the leather couch, trying to control the shaking that had set in now she was out of the public eye.

Her savior scrutinized her as if she might be dangerous. "Are you okay?"

She heard a wild quality in her laugh—no wonder he looked nervous. She took a deep, calming breath. "I've had better days."

"I'm sorry," he said. "I shouldn't have told you to go ahead with the wedding."

"I probably would have done it anyway." She ran a hand down her face, suddenly exhausted. "I'm the fool for agreeing to go on the program in the first place."

"I should have cancelled that stupid show the minute I heard of it."

A gruff voice said, "When you two have stopped arguing over who's to blame for this mess, you might want to think about how you're going to get out of it."

A middle-aged man, tall and trim, dressed conservatively in a dark suit and tie, had entered the room. Adam introduced him as Sam Magill, Channel Eight's in-house legal counsel and Adam's own attorney. The lawyer's sharp eyes narrowed to a point where Casey thought they might disappear.

"What you do in your private life is your business, Adam," he said. "But I'm amazed you'd get married without a prenup."

"Hey!" So what if it hadn't been a real wedding? Casey resented the implication she was after Adam's fortune, which presumably, since Sally Summers had described him as Memphis's most eligible bachelor, was considerable. "I'm not that kind of girl."

"Missy, everyone's that kind of girl when there's enough money involved," the lawyer said. "I don't like what happened to you back there, but if you plan on taking advantage of this situation to feather your own nest, I'm warning you—"

"That's enough, Sam," Adam said sharply. "That wasn't a real wedding, and as soon as Casey has a chance to work out where she's going next, I'll make an announcement to that effect."

The lawyer's jaw dropped. Then he broke into the wheezy laugh of a chronic smoker, a laugh that sent a tremor of unease through Casey.

"What's so funny?" Adam demanded.

It took a moment for Sam to regain his sober countenance. "Am I wrong, or was that David Dubois who performed that little ceremony out there?"

Adam nodded.

"The same David Dubois who served as a commissioner in Fayette County a couple of years back?"

Adam nodded again. "I believe he did."

"Then, my friend, I have news for you. The state of Tennessee allows marriages to be performed by any current or former county executive, as well as ministers, judges and the like." The lawyer cast his eyes to the ceiling as he spoke, as if reciting directly from Tennessee Code. "And unlike most other states, the executive doesn't have to have served in the county where the marriage is performed."

He brought his gaze back to Adam, a smile hovering on his lips. "For the rest of his life, your pal Dubois can legally marry anyone anywhere in Tennessee, as long as they have a marriage license." He paused, then delivered the coup de grâce. "You did get a license, didn't you?"

The wheezy laugh started again, and Casey knew the sound would haunt her for the rest of her days.

LEGALLY MARRIED. To a woman I don't know.

The irony wasn't lost on Adam as he held Casey's hand, waiting for the press conference to start. His reluctance to rush into marriage had opened the door to his relatives' lawsuit against him. If it was possible to laugh from beyond the grave, right now Adam's father would be in stitches.

Sorry, Dad, but this one won't last. The sooner Adam extricated them from this mess, and got his focus back on his real problems, the better. Sam Magill had already left to start working on an annulment.

"Keep Casey with you until you hear back from me," he had said on his way out the door. He was probably worried she would sneak off and open a joint checking account.

Adam had agreed, mainly because he'd been forced to scrap his plan of smuggling her out of the building, which was surrounded on all sides by media. Fortunately, Dave had slipped out before the press arrived.

Casey hadn't argued with the lawyer. She looked as if she was in shock, Adam thought. Her face, flushed with embarrassment in the studio, had paled to the same shade as her dress.

As many journalists as could fit were crammed into the Channel Eight lobby. Adam cursed the fact it was silly season—midsummer, when there wasn't enough news to fill the papers—which meant their wedding had attracted far more attention than it should have. He'd agreed to the press conference on the condition the journalists would allow them to leave privately afterward.

"I'll do the talking," he told Casey. His plan was to say as little as possible, to be noncommittal about their future until they knew where they stood legally. They would lie low for the weekend, and with any luck the fuss would have died down by

Monday. Hopefully, by the end of next week the announcement of their annulment would be absorbed by viewers over morning coffee, and his and Casey's brief alliance would soon be forgotten.

"*Kiss the Bride* is the hottest show in the land," the PR woman crowed to the media. "We're expecting huge demand from networks around the country…."

When she'd finished her spiel, she read out a hastily prepared statement from New Visage, which claimed to be delighted with the show and confident its relationship with Channel Eight would be both long and mutually beneficial.

That succeeded where nothing else could in putting a smile on Adam's face as he and Casey faced the barrage of camera flashes and the questions hurled at them.

"Mr. Carmichael, is this a ratings stunt?"

"Casey, why did you say yes?"

"Adam, how long do you give this marriage?"

"Are you in love?"

"Casey, what will your family think?"

At this last question, he felt the tremor of her fingers in his grasp. She looked imploringly at him. He held up a hand for silence.

"Ladies and gentlemen," he began, "as you've probably realized, tonight didn't go according to plan for either of us." Chuckles from the crowd told him they were on his side. All he had to do was give them enough to satisfy their immediate need for a

story, without exposing Casey to further humiliation and without actually lying. "We're asking you
to respect our privacy beyond what we tell you now.
I can reveal that Casey and I knew each other before
this evening's show—" only an hour before, admittedly "—and that for as long as I've known her I've
considered her a very special lady."

Any grown woman who could cling to her dream
of being adored had to be special.

He looked down at Casey, noting that a few
tendrils of honey-colored hair had escaped her veil.
Gratitude warmed her eyes, and her lips curved in
a tremulous smile. He turned back to the waiting
media. "Can you blame me for seizing the chance
to marry her?"

Applause broke out among the journalists.
Pleased at the success of his speech, Adam grinned
at Casey. She smiled back, obviously relieved.

"Hey, Mr. C." It was one of the older hacks.
"How about you kiss the bride?"

Photographers readied their cameras in a flurry
of motion.

Adam raised his eyebrows in silent question to
Casey. She gave a barely perceptible shrug, then a
nod.

Once again, their lips met.

Like last time, he intended a brief kiss, one that
would allow the cameras to get their shot.

Like last time, he found himself drawn to her.

Despite the crowd around them, he couldn't resist the temptation to test the softness of her lower lip with his tongue. Her indrawn breath told him she was just as intrigued by the exploration.

The catcalls of the journalists pulled them both back to reality.

"Okay, folks, that's all." Mainly with the power of his glare, but using his elbows where necessary, Adam parted the throng and ushered Casey out the front of the building and into a waiting limo. She scrambled across to the far side, gathering her skirts about her to make room for him.

"Where to now?" Casey asked. The last half hour had passed in a blur, and she couldn't imagine what might come next. All she knew was it couldn't be worse than what had happened in the studio.

Adam's half smile held equal measures of cynicism and resignation. "Our honeymoon."

CHAPTER THREE

IT WAS TEN O'CLOCK at night—her wedding night—by the time they got to the Romeo and Juliet Suite at Memphis's famous Peabody Hotel.

Casey—or Mrs. Carmichael, as the hotel receptionist had called her—roamed around the room, while Adam tipped the porter. The original honeymoon Channel Eight offered hadn't included the suite, which Casey suspected went for several hundred dollars a night. But a standard hotel room wasn't going to work for a newly married couple who had no intention of sharing a bedroom, let alone a bed.

Judging by the crowd of reporters who'd followed them from the TV station, and were now being held at bay by the Peabody's doorman—so much for their promise to respect the newlyweds' privacy—Casey and Adam wouldn't be leaving the hotel in a hurry, so the bigger the suite the better. Casey climbed the curving staircase to the bedroom. The king-size bed was a sea of snowy-white covers and elaborately arranged pillows. Surely a real honeymoon couple would want something cozier?

There was a bathroom off the bedroom, in addition to the one she'd seen adjoining the living room. More white—marble and porcelain—offset by highly polished stainless steel fittings.

"Casey?" Adam called from downstairs.

Dreading having to sit down and hash out the legal implications of what they'd done, she joined him in the living room. How was she going to explain this to her family? How would she respond when they demanded her immediate return to Parkvale?

Right now, she doubted she could resist. The newfound backbone that had empowered her to seize control of her future had crumbled when Joe jilted her. She would get it back; of course she would. But not tonight.

"It's late," Adam said. "You must be exhausted. How about we get some sleep and talk in the morning, when we've heard back from Sam about the annulment?"

"Sounds perfect." At least she'd married a man who didn't expect her to solve all their problems.

"You take the bedroom, this couch will do me."

Considerate, too. Casey wasn't about to argue. She tried but failed to stifle a yawn. "Thanks, Adam." She ran a hand around the back of her neck to ease muscles exhausted from the strain of holding her head high through today's fiasco. "Good night."

A knock at the door interrupted his reply. Adam opened it and a bellboy presented him with an envelope. Casey caught a glimpse of the words *Private and Confidential.*

"From Sam," Adam said.

Thank goodness. Hopefully the lawyer had figured a way out of this predicament.

Adam tore it open. It took him only a second to read the contents. He uttered a half laugh, half groan.

"What is it? Bad news?"

He didn't answer, only gave her a brooding look.

She stretched out a hand. "May I see it?"

He held the note just out of her reach. "I'm not sure you want to."

In answer, she snatched it from him. And read Sam Magill's instruction, etched on the fine paper in bold blue strokes.

DO NOT CONSUMMATE THE MARRIAGE.

"Oh." Casey dropped it on the coffee table, her cheeks burning. "As if we were going to. That's… that's…"

"Ridiculous?"

"Exactly."

"Sam is very thorough. I imagine he wanted to cover all contingencies." Adam grinned, and that furrow of tension disappeared. "Perhaps he was worried by your enthusiasm when you kissed me at the TV studio."

Casey sputtered. "*I* kissed *you?* You're the one

who heated things up." The memory of his mouth on hers flooded back, leaving her light-headed. She clutched at the only possible explanation. "It was a rebound thing for me."

That wiped the smile off Adam's face. He looked pointedly toward the couch. "I think it's time we got some sleep. Separately."

In the bedroom, Casey discovered the reason why someone else had buttoned her dress for her at the TV studio. There must have been at least thirty tiny pearl buttons down her back, most of them beyond her reach.

She grappled with the dress for another minute, but it was hopeless. Peeking down into the living room, she was relieved to find Adam hadn't yet gone to bed, he stood by the window, staring out over Union Avenue, deep in thought.

Casey headed down the stairs. "Adam? I can't undo my buttons. Could you help?"

She half turned her back so he could see the problem, and he came to her aid.

Casey had never realized the area between her shoulder blades, where the buttons started, was so sensitive. The brush of Adam's fingers against her bare skin stimulated a whole bunch of nerve endings. She shivered.

"Cold?" he asked, his tone impersonal.

Casey nodded, holding herself rigid to prevent any more of those traitorous shivers. But it didn't lessen the sensation. She felt the release of each little button, aware that more and more of her flesh was showing. Warmth rose within her—was it possible her back was blushing?

This had to be because of that note from the lawyer. They'd been told not to consummate the marriage, and five minutes later she'd had to ask Adam to undress her.

"You can probably manage the rest yourself," he said, his voice clipped.

She stepped away. "Thanks. I hope you won't be too uncomfortable on that thing." She gestured to the couch.

He looked at her for a long moment, then his gaze dropped to her shoulders. He said tightly, "Time you were in bed."

DESPITE HER EXHAUSTION, Casey slept badly. All that subterfuge, her humiliation aired on national TV, the extreme step of marrying a stranger, and she was no better off than when she had left Parkvale on Friday morning. Her family would be frantic to know what was going on. But perhaps the worst thing was that she hadn't even thought about Joe since he'd run out on her, aside from a brief urge as she left the stage to murder him by the most violent means possible.

That compulsion had passed, leaving a curious void.

It took no great psychological insight to realize how little Joe really meant to her. How could she have planned to marry him? She'd convinced herself she could give him the no-strings love she wanted for herself, when really she was using him to get away from her family.

In hindsight, she deserved to be dumped. Perhaps not quite so publicly…but she'd brought that on herself.

Casey allowed the recriminations to chase around in her head as she lay in bed until eight o'clock, when she was sure Adam would have had time to get dressed. She showered, then looked in her suitcase at the clothes she'd packed for her honeymoon. She'd bought a couple of new items, skimpier than she would normally wear, with the idea, she supposed now, of turning Joe on.

She rejected a strappy top in favor of a white, sleeveless T-shirt, which she teamed with a denim skirt. She checked her reflection in the full-length mirror. No way could Adam think she'd dressed to turn him on.

He was standing at the dining table when she got downstairs. Someone must have brought his luggage during the night. He wore jeans and a black polo shirt, open at the neck. Casey's gaze was drawn to his bare forearms, tanned and strong, as he lifted the covers off several dishes on a room-service trolley. He pulled a chair out for her, and

Casey wiped her palms against the sturdy fabric of her skirt as she sat down.

"I ordered breakfast," he said. "It's not safe to go down to the restaurant. The manager tells me a couple of journalists checked into the hotel."

Casey helped herself to fruit and yogurt, shaking her head at Adam's offer of a hot meal. He piled his own plate with scrambled eggs, bacon and toast, raised his glass of orange juice to her in salute, and started on his breakfast.

Casey took a sip of her own juice as she glanced at the newspaper that lay folded by her plate—and promptly choked.

"Oh, no." After all those photos she and Adam had posed for at the press conference, they'd published one taken in the TV studio, obviously at the moment Joe had jilted her. Her face, panic in her eyes, mouth open, gaped back at her from the front page beneath the headline Carmichael Rescues Jilted Bride. She grabbed a napkin, wiped away the rivulet of juice she could feel on her chin, without taking her eyes off the newspaper.

"It's not as bad as it looks." Adam was presumably referring to the article and not to her photo, because that couldn't be any worse. "They speculate that Channel Eight cooked up this scheme to boost the ratings of *Kiss the Bride*. They tried to get a comment out of your fiancé, but he wasn't talking."

Casey unfolded the paper, then clamped a hand to

her forehead at the sight of her father, peering around the front door of the house. "They spoke to my dad."

"That's not so good," Adam admitted. "They also talked to my stepmother. Seems she told them we've been secretly engaged for months."

"Why would she say that?"

Adam shrugged. "My guess is she didn't want to be caught not knowing about something as important as my wedding." Casey gathered from the careful neutrality of his expression that he didn't much like his stepmother. "Still, she's probably helped confuse the press, which can't hurt."

"Any word from the lawyer?" Casey asked.

"I've had a few calls." He gestured to the cell phone on the table between them. "But not from Sam."

His phone trilled again.

"Hello, Eloise," he said with resigned patience. "Did you like the show?"

Who was Eloise? His stepmother? His girlfriend?

Whoever she was, Adam was obviously enjoying her reaction to their wedding. Not his girlfriend, then. He grinned and held the phone away from his ear—Casey heard a spate of words pouring out. "Sorry, Eloise, I have another call coming through. I'll get back to you."

That set the pattern for the next few minutes, with Adam receiving one call after another, mostly, she gathered, from family, all anxious to know how his marriage might affect their interests. His reticence must have infuriated them.

Bored with waiting, Casey turned on her own cell phone. Almost immediately, it beeped with a text message from the answering service to say she had twenty-one new messages.

She dialed the service and scrolled through the worried communications from her father (five messages), her sister (six) and her brother (one). There was also one from Brodie-Ann, and several from people who were concerned her wedding might make Casey unavailable to help them. People like the church choir director (did the wedding mean she wouldn't be singing her solo this Sunday?) and the head of the Parkvale Children's Trust (Casey was still okay to bake two cakes and a batch of cookies for next week's open day, wasn't she?).

No and no. She couldn't help smiling. She'd figured getting married would give her the perfect out, but not like this. Still, she wouldn't call anyone back just yet. Not until she and Adam had talked. His phone rang again, and she sighed. Whenever that might be. She realized she hadn't touched her food yet, and took a mouthful of yogurt-smothered melon.

Then her own phone rang, chirping "You Are My Sunshine." By the time she'd convinced the Parkvale librarian she wasn't available to fill in during children's story hour that afternoon, Adam was off the phone and regarding her quizzically.

"Did your phone just play 'You Are My Sunshine'?" he asked.

"Uh-huh. It's a personalized ring tone. It's affirming."

He laughed, until the dignified raising of her eyebrows told him she was serious.

"Affirmations are good for your self-esteem," she told him. "Every time my phone tells me I'm its sunshine, it makes me feel good." Though at this precise moment it didn't seem to be working. Still, she gave Adam a sunny smile as she popped another piece of melon into her mouth.

"You really believe that?"

She nodded. "You have to find an affirmation that works for you, of course. 'You Are My Sunshine' gives me confidence." Casey thought about that furrow that had made a permanent home in Adam's brow. "Whereas you might want to look in your mirror each morning and tell yourself you won't get stressed today."

He frowned, and the furrow deepened. "I hope you didn't pay good money to learn that psychobabble."

"That comes direct from my community college lecturer," she protested.

"I'll bet he didn't tell you to get affirmation from your cell phone."

"No, *she* didn't. I'm extrapolating."

Adam tackled his bacon and eggs, which must surely be cold after all those phone calls, with renewed energy. "So why are you studying psychology? To overcome childhood trauma?"

"I'm not in therapy," she said with exaggerated patience. "I study psychology because it helps with characterization in my writing." Her phone warbled again and she looked at the display. "It's my dad."

Her father took a moment to remind her he loved her, then launched into a monologue about how much her family needed her and how she'd better sort out this confusion and get back home as soon as possible. He ended with a plaintive query: "How am I supposed to get to physical therapy on Tuesday?"

Call a cab. Don't you think I have more on my mind right now? But she'd taught her father she would always be there when he needed her, so how could she blame him? She was saved from answering by a beep on the line.

"Just a moment, Dad, I have another call." She switched to the other line.

Her sister. Casey straightened in her seat. "Yes, Karen, I did just get married. No, I'm not crazy—" she hoped that wasn't a lie "—and no, I'm not coming back to Parkvale." She hoped that wasn't a lie, either. "I'd like you and Dad to— Hello?"

When she got back to the other line, her father wasn't there.

"Bad connection," she explained to Adam. She put her phone on the gilded, glass-topped table between them and looked hard at her plate so he wouldn't see the hurt she knew must show in her face. "Now that we're both free—"

"Free being a relative term," he interrupted. "We're still married."

"—let's have that chat you mentioned." Her phone rang again, but after a glance at the display she ignored it.

"You could always turn that thing off," Adam said. His own phone rang, and he answered it. Which at least gave Casey a chance to regain her fighting spirit.

"You were saying?" she asked sweetly, when he'd finished.

He frowned. "I'm expecting a call from Sam. I don't want to miss it."

"And I need to talk to my family," she said. "Even though I don't know what to tell them."

There was a moment's silence. Then Casey's phone chirped "You Are My Sunshine" again.

"Karen, please, honey, don't cry." Casey's voice wobbled. "I'm sorry, I know you wanted me there, but this is for your own good, sweetie."

Adam realized Casey was blinking in an effort to hold back tears. Rising hysteria emanated from her cell phone, audible even to him, several feet away.

He checked his watch. If she was going to spend the whole morning arguing with her family, they'd never get this mess sorted out. From what he could see, her folks were as bad as his own relatives. There was only one way to deal with people like that. Get tough.

One look at Casey told him that wasn't going to happen. In two seconds, Adam had moved around the table and slipped the phone from her grasp—easily done, since she wasn't expecting it.

"Karen? I don't know who you are, but you're not helping Casey right now." He crossed the room, aware of Casey's startled expression. Karen sputtered on the other end of the phone.

"My *wife* and I—" damn, that sounded weird "—need some time alone." He reached the huge vase filled with an elaborate display of flowers, delivered last night compliments of the Peabody management. Casey, following right behind, bumped into him. "So goodbye."

With Karen still squawking, he dropped the phone—right into the vase.

Casey yelped. "Have you gone crazy?"

"You're not prepared to turn that thing off, and it's upsetting you. I'm dealing with the problem." He dusted his hands together. "Doesn't that feel better?"

"No! How could you…" She stopped. "Actually," she said slowly, "it does." She ventured a small smile.

From across the room they heard the sound of his phone.

"Allow me to deal with that." Casey moved toward it.

"It's okay." He followed her. "I'll take it."

She'd picked it up already and was reading the display. "It's Eloise."

"My stepmother again." He rolled his eyes. "Pass it here."

"I said I'd deal with it," Casey reminded him. She stepped back and moved around the other side of the sofa.

Adam wasn't quite sure what happened next. But somehow, he went one way and she went the other, toward the open window.

"Casey, don't—"

Too late.

She dropped the phone just as he reached her.

Adam looked so shocked, Casey wondered if she'd gone too far. She held her breath as he stuck his head out the window. When he turned back into the room, his face was grave. "You just killed an Elvis impersonator."

Casey clapped a hand to her mouth. "No! I looked, there was no one—" Then she caught the grin he was trying to hide.

And they were laughing, clinging to each other in helpless hilarity that for a moment made the whole mess go away.

Adam looked into Casey's eyes, where tears of merriment glistened. On automatic pilot, he wiped the corner of her eye with his thumb. And found himself robbed of all sensation except the pressing desire to feel her mouth beneath his.

CHAPTER FOUR

THAT TOUCH OF HIS THUMB seemed to wipe away Casey's mirth. Her gray eyes widened and her teeth caught her bottom lip. After the tiniest of hesitations she swayed against him.

This time, there was no tentative overture on his part—and no audience to inhibit the eager parting of her lips to admit him.

Kissing her, Adam told himself as he claimed her mouth, was a reaction to the stress of the past twenty-four hours.

Then her tongue met his with a fervor that matched his own, she wound her arms around his neck and he gave up trying to justify his actions. Gave himself up to the sensual pleasure of kissing Casey, to the press of her body against his, to his own undeniable physical reaction. He cupped her firm derriere, pulling her closer. With a murmur of surprise, she arched into him.

If he didn't stop now, they'd be in danger of complicating this disaster beyond repair.

Tearing his mouth from hers took a degree of

willpower he didn't ever recall needing with a woman. When at last they stood apart, Adam ran a hand through his hair as if that might erase the memory of her touch there. He made a conscious effort to slow his breathing. Casey's cheeks were flushed, her lips still parted in what looked to him like invitation.

"Adam." Breathlessness made her breasts rise and fall, her voice husky. "You have *got* to stop doing that."

Okay, maybe not invitation.

She turned away, gazed with studied casualness at a framed photograph on the wall, a shot of downtown Memphis at night. "Not that it wasn't nice," she said. "But…you know."

Yes, he knew it was a dumb idea to get distracted from fixing this catastrophe. But she'd enjoyed that kiss as much as he had, so he was damned if he was going to apologize.

At the sound of rustling, they turned to the door. A piece of paper had been slid underneath.

Adam picked it up and scanned it. "It's a message from Sam. He's at home and ready to take my call." He'd instructed the hotel reception not to put any calls through to their suite. He reached for the phone on the sideboard next to the dining table and started dialing.

Casey took the opportunity to move as far away from him as she could. She plunked herself on the blue-and-gold-striped couch, grabbed up the room service menu from the coffee table and held it open so Adam couldn't see her face. Her red face.

Good grief, she'd acted like a sex-starved wanton, wrapping herself around him that way. She'd be the first to admit that her sex life with Joe had been rather lackluster the past few years—and nonexistent for nearly a year—but that was no excuse to throw herself at the first man she met. Even if he was her *husband*.

From behind the menu, she listened shamelessly to Adam's side of the conversation with Sam. Which didn't tell her much; he was a man of few words. When he'd finished, he dropped the receiver back into its cradle. He muttered something under his breath that Casey didn't quite hear, but it didn't sound like, "Yippee, we got our annulment."

"Is there a problem?" she asked.

He came to the couch, stood over her with his hands jammed into the pockets of his jeans, his eyebrows drawn together. "Getting an annulment will be difficult."

Casey gulped. "How difficult?"

"They're something of a rarity in Tennessee. There's no statutory basis for annulment here. Each case has to be argued on common law principles."

"Meaning?"

"Meaning," he said, "there's no official annulment process. My lawyer will put a case together and argue it before a judge. If the judge agrees, we get our annulment."

"And if the judge doesn't agree?"

"We get a divorce."

"But I don't want to be divorced," Casey protested.

"Right now, I'd rather be divorced than married," he said, with a flat finality that prickled the back of her neck. He sat down on the couch opposite, saving her the strain of looking up at him. "Sam tells me he can make a good case for annulment. Nonconsummation of the marriage is a definite plus. Even stronger is the fact we didn't know it was a real wedding. Still, some of those old judges take marriage pretty seriously." Cynicism twisted his mouth. "Sam wants to make sure he gets a sympathetic judge, and that might take up to a month."

"So we'll be married for a month," Casey said, "and then it'll be as if it never happened."

"Exactly."

"Everything will be just the same as before."

"Uh-huh."

"Nothing will have changed. *Nothing.*"

"Yes," Adam said impatiently. Didn't she understand plain English?

"No," she said.

Adam's head hurt. "What's that supposed to mean?"

"I'm not going back to Parkvale. I'm done with that place."

"You can go wherever you like," he said. *The sooner the better.*

"They'll make me go back." Her eyes flickered toward the door.

He'd married a paranoiac.

She stood and paced to the window. There was something hunted about the way she put her palms against the glass. Staring out into the distance, she said desperately, "Can't we—can't we just stay married?"

A *delusional* paranoiac.

Keep her calm, Adam told himself. *Talk up the joys of a future on her own, then get Sam here fast with some kind of agreement for her to sign, relinquishing all claim on me.*

She turned around, perched that derriere he'd enjoyed caressing—*that was before I knew she was nuts*—on the windowsill. "Stop looking like I'm about to jump you." She folded her arms under her breasts. "I didn't mean it about staying married. Even if the past twenty-four hours hadn't totally turned me off wedded bliss, you're not my type."

He didn't believe that for a second, not after the way she'd kissed him. He started in on the keep-her-calm stuff. "No one can make you go anywhere," he soothed. "You have your whole life ahead of you."

"You don't know my family," she said gloomily. Her eyes narrowed as she looked at Adam. "Your in-laws."

His instantaneous recoil made her giggle.

"They're not that bad," she said. "I've just kind

of overdosed on them. I've looked after Dad—and Karen and Mike, my sister and brother—since Mom died when I was twelve. I'm the oldest, so I ended up taking care of the house, the cooking, everything."

"Very commendable," Adam said politely.

She looked dubious. "It wasn't like I had a choice. They needed me. Not that I minded," she said hastily. "I love them to bits."

"You don't have to go back just because you didn't marry Joe."

"I'm a pushover," she said with the confessional air of someone about to embark on a twelve-step program. "When I tried to leave home and go to college, Dad convinced me the others needed me while they were still in high school. Then I was all set to leave after Mike graduated, but Dad got injured in an accident at work. He was in the hospital for six months, in a wheelchair for a year. He's better now, but he needed a lot of help, and I was the logical candidate."

"You could have left once he was better."

She leaned her head back against the window. "Like I said, I'm a pushover. Dad's become dependent on me. For his sake, he needs to learn to look after himself again. If I'd married Joe and moved away like we planned, Dad wouldn't have a choice. Now he'll insist I go back, and Karen will be right there with him, putting in her two cents' worth."

"Does she still live at home?"

Casey shook her head. "She was a lawyer in Dallas until she had a baby a few months ago. But she just separated from her husband, and she's moving home to Parkvale. She wants to go back to work and leave Rosie with me. She says she wouldn't trust a nanny."

Casey didn't tell Adam how Karen's letter had filled her with equal parts longing and dread. Dread because once again her plan to leave home would be thwarted. But even greater, and unexpected, had been Casey's longing to lavish all her maternal love on her sister's baby—love that might otherwise go unused.

Adam walked over to the window. He stood so close to her she could have reached out and touched him. "Just tell them no."

"Haven't you ever said yes to someone when you didn't want to?" she demanded.

"I don't do anything I don't want to do," he said starkly.

She blinked. "Well, that's nice for you. But I just can't say no to all that...that—"

"Emotional blackmail?" he suggested.

Casey nodded. Maybe, despite his uncompromising claim, he did understand. Back when Mom died, Casey had been the only one who could do what had to be done. She'd done so without knowing it would become a trap of her own making, a mutual dependence none of them could escape. Because being needed had a seductive appeal all its own. Which made *not* being needed tantamount to a withdrawal of love.

It was screwy, but somehow she'd fallen into that way of thinking.

Even her relationship with Joe had been built on need and dependence. Joe's mom had left him when he was a kid. He needed a woman who would stick with him forever. He didn't mind that Casey might never have a baby of her own, if the doctors were right; Joe would've been happy not to share her with a child. Or so she had thought.

"A couple of months ago, I won a writing contest with part of a young adult novel I'm writing," she told Adam. "The editor who judged it wants to see the whole book. She's speaking at a conference in Dallas in August. I arranged to meet her there and give her my manuscript." She sighed. "If I go home, I'll never finish it. My family sees my writing as a hobby, and every volunteer organization in Parkvale has me down as a soft touch."

To Adam, writing a book sounded like another girlish fantasy. It ranked right up there with being adored. She needed to stop dreaming and start doing something that would halt the emotional blackmail. Like Adam was. Though in his case, the blackmail was as physical as it was emotional.

And in his case, blackmail wouldn't work. He'd meant it when he told Casey he didn't do anything he didn't want to. That was why his dad had gone to such extreme lengths when he'd made his will, a last-ditch attempt to make Adam do what his father wanted.

It was ironic that despite the differences between them, he and Casey were both struggling with pressure from their families. Ironic that if their marriage had been real, it would have solved both their problems....

The idea burst into blazing, clamoring life.

"You're right," he said. "We should stay married."

"What?" She slipped off the windowsill, grabbing for the curtain tieback to steady herself. "I'm sure you're very nice—" she didn't sound at all sure, he noticed "—but I'm not desperate enough to stay married to a stranger."

His eyes narrowed. "You were desperate enough to lie to your fiancé and marry him on a reality-TV show."

"I was bringing the wedding *forward,*" she said. "We were *engaged.*"

"And we—" with a wave of his hand he indicated the two of them "—are married." He paced between the window and the couch as he thought about how they could make this work. "I don't mean we'd be married for real. We'd just stay together until the annulment comes through. For a month, we pretend we're truly husband and wife. In public," he added hastily.

"I can see that might help me," she admitted. "But how does it help you?"

Adam figured he'd have to tell her enough to convince her. "When my father died, he left me his majority share of Carmichael Broadcasting. His will stipulated that if I'm not married—or as he put it, in a marriage of a lasting and committed nature—when I'm thirty, my share passes to my cousin Henry."

"Is that legal, demanding that someone be married in order to inherit?"

Adam shrugged as he leaned against the back of the couch. "No. At least Sam says it's not. But the will stands until we make a case in court to prove it's invalid. Sam and I are working on that now. But Henry and his mother, my aunt Anna May, have their lawyers working to prove the will *is* legal. They're hoping Henry will inherit. They know I'd never get married just to please my father."

"Sounds like your dad was a real romantic," Casey said. She caught a glint of irritation in Adam's eyes.

"Dad had reason to believe I was anti-marriage. I admit that when he died, getting married was the last thing on my mind. But I assumed I'd find someone suitable over the next few years."

Someone suitable? Did he mean someone he loved? "But you didn't," she guessed.

"I was wrong." He shoved his hands into his pockets. "I turn thirty next month. If the will's ruled legal, I'll have until I turn thirty-one to find a wife. My stepmother's not so confident we can have it overturned. She'd like me to get married, so that I win either way. She's spent the past few months arranging *accidental* introductions to the daughters of her friends. She's organizing a party for my birthday, and I know she's planning on inviting practically every woman in Memphis. I don't have time for this crap—I have a business to run and a lawsuit to fight. But with Eloise, my life is turning into one long *bridefest*." He poured loathing into the word.

"Hey," Casey protested. "This sounds just like my family. If you don't do anything you don't want to, how come you don't just tell Eloise to take a hike?"

"I wish I could," Adam said with feeling. "Before Dad died, he asked me to take care of her. I *want* to honor his memory, to keep my promise. But she makes it damn hard."

"Were she and your father close?"

Anger flickered in his eyes, then vanished. "You could say my father died for her." The look he gave Casey said, *Don't ask.*

Briefly, she considered asking anyway. But that might be pushing her luck—and she still didn't understand why Adam wanted to pretend their marriage was genuine. She abandoned her position at the window to return to the couch. "So you want to beat your aunt's lawsuit and you want to escape Eloise's bridefest." She spoke the word with relish, and he glared.

"If I'm married, she'll have to back off. No more introductions, no birthday party. Anna May and Henry will think they've lost the battle because I've already met the will's conditions. By the time the annulment comes through and they realize they were wrong, Sam and I will have built a compelling case against the will."

Adam spread his hands, palms up, as if to say this was unarguable logic. "So what say we buy ourselves some time? A month is long enough for me to deter Eloise and get my legal battle under control. Is it enough for your sister and your father to sort out their problems? You can use the computer at my place to work on your book, since you'll have nothing else to do."

He smiled and Casey's danger sensors went on alert. This man was used to getting what he wanted, and she suspected he might ride roughshod over others to get it.

"It could be just what you dreamed of, a no-strings marriage," he added.

She'd dreamed of no-strings love.

"It sounds selfish," she said, trying to imagine lying to her family just so she could stay away from them.

"Exactly," Adam said with satisfaction. "This is all about being selfish for once in your life." He regarded her doubtfully. "I suspect you're no good at it, but I'll show you how. Then, when our time is up, we'll go our separate ways. No demands on each other, no...*neediness.*" He all but shuddered at the word, and in that moment Casey decided to grab with both hands the opportunity he presented.

"You're right." She felt a sudden, blissful lightening of her gloom, and sprang to her feet. "I'm sick of being needed. Let's do it, Adam. Let's be selfish."

"Utterly, totally, one hundred percent selfish." He smiled broadly, and that furrow in his brow turned into a laugh line, making him look younger, almost carefree.

He put out a hand to shake on the deal. By now, the buzz of electricity his touch produced was so familiar, Casey could almost persuade herself to ignore it.

But could she ignore it for a whole month?

CHAPTER FIVE

ELOISE CARMICHAEL DIDN'T let her hesitation show in her walk. Sam Magill had eyes in the back of his head where she was concerned. She wouldn't put it past him to have sensed her arrival and be watching her progress up his front path on this fine Sunday afternoon.

She wouldn't want him to get the wrong idea about her turning up at his house uninvited. She stiffened her spine and took brisk, businesslike steps, which wasn't easy wearing delicate high-heeled pumps in the green silk-linen fabric that matched her suit.

She pressed the brass doorbell near the wide front door and waited, clutching her green kid leather purse in front of her.

Sam opened the door. He blinked twice in astonishment, making his face seem even more owlish than usual. Then a flush crept up his cheeks from somewhere below his chin. Today, that predictable reaction was a relief, not an embarrassment. Because Eloise was here to take advantage of Sam's…interest in her.

He smiled warmly. "Eloise, what an unexpected pleasure."

She had to admit it was nice to know at least one man was always happy to see her. Sam's regard went some small way toward countering all the frosty welcomes she'd endured from her stepson over the years.

"What can I do for you?" That catch phrase prefaced their every conversation.

Eloise wondered if the man had ever heard of "Good afternoon" or "How are you today?" He was still smiling, hopefully now.

She shouldn't have come. She dropped her gaze from the transparent eagerness of his expression. Then blinked. He was wearing bedroom slippers on his feet! Brown-and-cream checked ones that had seen better days, judging by the pilling at the toes. Eloise drew in a breath. It was silly to be shocked, but James would *never* have answered the door in his slippers.

James is gone.

"I need to talk to you about Adam," she said, the wobble in her voice part grief at the reminder of what she'd lost, but mainly anxiety for her stepson. "I should have called first, but I thought you might refuse to see me."

"Refuse… No, of course… Why would I?" Sam stepped back to let her in. He stumbled against an Oriental pot used as an umbrella stand and it toppled over, spilling two neatly furled black umbrellas onto the polished floorboards. "Oh, dear, just let me—" He bent to retrieve the umbrellas, and when he stood up, dislodged a hat hanging on a row of pegs on the wall.

Sam had never looked twice at Eloise during her marriage, nor in those early years after James's death. But for three years now, he'd had this crush on her. He knocked things over, blurted tactless remarks, blushed to the roots of his hair—just like a teenage boy, minus the acne.

Knowing it would take him half a minute to regain his composure, Eloise waited in silence while he stumbled over words and furnishings.

She valued loyalty, so she appreciated that his attachment to her never wavered. But she wished she wasn't too much of a lady to tell him bluntly there was no point. That she didn't need or want anyone if she couldn't have James.

Blast you, James Carmichael, for leaving me a widow. Do you know how lonely I feel every day? Every night?

When Sam was coherent and no longer in immediate danger of destroying anything, she followed him into the living room.

She'd never been to this house before, and now she looked around with curiosity. Leather couches and chunky wooden tables stamped a masculine seal on the high-ceilinged room. A deep-piled rug in chocolate-brown warmed the floor, and book-shelves lined the walls.

The room was comfortable, uncluttered. Expensive. Adam often said Sam had the sharpest legal brain in Memphis. In these surroundings, Eloise could almost believe there was another side to the man, beyond his bumbling adoration.

She moved toward the nearest couch, and a sudden prickling in her throat made her cough. Now she smelled a familiar, spicy aroma, saw the faint blue haze that hung over the coffee table.

Sam caught the direction of her gaze. "Let me get rid of that." He pushed aside the newspaper spread across the table, and reached for his cigar, grinding the lighted tip into the cut-glass ashtray until it looked quite dead.

"Thank you," Eloise said. She waited for him to offer her a seat.

But Sam was looking her up and down, taking in her fitted mint-green suit and ivory silk blouse with an overtness that surprised her. "That's a very nice outfit, Eloise. You look…crisp and, uh, fresh."

Gracious, the man has no idea. Small wonder he'd never found himself a wife. "You make me sound like an apple."

He blushed again. "I'm sorry," he said, "I meant to say you look…you look…" The hunger in his eyes dismayed Eloise.

Mercy. "I can't stay long, I'm on my way out for

dinner," she said. He appeared so alarmed, she had to add, "At a girlfriend's house."

"You look sensational," he blurted, as if he'd just found the right word. "And those shoes are perfect."

Call her vain, but Eloise couldn't help smiling. "You know, Sam," she said, "next time you meet an attractive, unattached lady, you should try paying her a compliment like that. You'll be amazed at the results."

"But you're an—"

"May we talk about Adam now, please?" she said firmly.

At last, he showed her to a seat, and took the leather recliner next to her.

Eloise crossed her legs at the ankles, and strove for the right blend of command and entreaty. "I need to know about this wedding. I spoke to Adam on his cell phone, but he wouldn't talk—you know how he gets. Now he's not answering at all. Tell me what's going on, Sam."

Patently uncomfortable, the lawyer ran a hand through his iron-gray hair. "Adam is…married."

She tightened her grip on her purse. "But who is she? How long has he known her? Does he love her?" Eloise heard the rise in her voice as she asked the questions that had kept her awake the past two nights. She drew a deep breath. "Sam, I'm worried my pressuring him to find a wife might have driven Adam to do something foolish."

Sam shifted in his seat, clearly agitated. Eloise could see he wanted to help her, but his voice was firm when he said, "Adam's my client. You know I can't tell you that."

She flashed her most charming smile. "Now, Sam, we're friends. At least tell me if the woman is nice. Does she love Adam?" Eloise swallowed. "I can't bear the thought of someone else latching on to Adam for what she can get." Not after what the poor boy was going through with his aunt and his cousin. "Tell me at least if you made her sign a prenup."

Still surprisingly unmoved, Sam spread his hands. "I'm not at liberty to say."

"Does his marriage mean Anna May's lawsuit won't get anywhere?" Eloise pressed. If Adam had traded one grasping woman for another, he might at least come out even.

Sam coughed for several long seconds, with the apparent intention of ignoring her question.

"Don't think your smoker's cough lets you off the hook," she said reprovingly. "Maybe you can't talk about Adam, but you can about Anna May."

But Sam remained annoyingly reticent. "Hmm, you know your sister-in-law."

Which Eloise did, only too well. James's sister clung to Henry, her son, in a way that had stopped the boy growing into a man with any decent backbone. Not like Adam—so independent, so strong-minded. Of course, sometimes it would be nice if Adam would allow just a tiny bit of clinging. Eloise's relationship with him was the polar opposite of Anna May's with Henry.

"Just take me to see him. Please, Sam, you're my friend." Oh dear, she hadn't meant to reach out and clasp his hand where it rested on the arm of his recliner. It was the sort of gesture she wouldn't think twice about with one of her girlfriends, but with Sam… The feel of his fingers beneath hers distracted her, and for a moment she tightened her grip. How long had it been since she'd touched roughened male skin? *Oh, James, James.*

Sam's face was brick-red as he extricated his hand. He stood up. "James was one of my closest friends," he said, and for a moment she thought he'd read her thoughts. "I count Adam a good friend, too. But you and I both know you don't see me as a friend, Eloise."

She felt heat in her cheeks and was about to contradict him when he said fiercely, "And we both know I don't think of you as just a friend."

Eloise scrambled off the couch, less elegantly than she'd have liked. She stared at Sam, uncertain.

But the fire left him as suddenly as it had blazed. "If there's anything else I can do…" he said mildly. "Maybe drive you to your dinner tonight? If you plan on drinking wine I could fetch you afterward…."

It was the sort of offer he was always making,

implying she was incompetent. "I am perfectly capable of driving myself." Eloise drew herself up to her full five feet seven—which suddenly didn't feel tall enough—and said with all the imperiousness she could summon, "You asked what you could do for me. I told you, and you refused. Don't ever say those hollow words to me again."

As she swept from the room, she said over her shoulder, "You, Sam Magill, are no gentleman."

"ADAM," CASEY SAID on Sunday afternoon. "Are we rich and famous?"

Adam looked up from the newspaper. Casey was sitting on the couch, along with…was that the hotel maid sitting next to her, face blotchy and eyes puffy?

"We?" he said cautiously.

"Mr. and Mrs. Adam Carmichael."

He flinched, and she grinned.

"Why do you ask?" The maid was definitely crying, sniveling into a handkerchief that looked suspiciously like one of Adam's. Casey was clasping the girl's free hand.

Whatever was going on, Adam knew he wasn't going to like it.

"I mean," Casey said, "do people do as you tell them?"

"Usually." Everyone except his family.

"Great." Casey turned to the maid. "Don't worry, Ria, we'll help you."

The girl sobbed something incoherent in Spanish.

"Casey…" Adam murmured. Her eyes met his, wide with innocent inquiry. He jerked his head meaningfully at the maid. Counting on the girl not understanding, or being too upset to listen, he said, "Emotional blackmail."

Casey bristled. "Poor Ria hasn't seen her fiancé in six months. He doesn't have a U.S. work permit, so he's stuck in Mexico. I'd be crying, too."

"Did she ask you to help?" The girl had a nerve—Adam would complain to the hotel management.

"Of course not," Casey said, affronted on the maid's behalf. "I offered."

That was even worse.

"What happened to being selfish?" he demanded.

"I can't be *that* selfish."

"This—" he meant their plan "—won't work if you don't."

Before he could stop her, Casey phoned the manager and invited him up to the suite. When he arrived, she asked him to apply for a work permit for the maid's boyfriend and give him a job. "My husband and I would be so grateful," she said, with what Adam conceded was an impressively straight face. And when the manager appeared less than willing, she grasped his hands and pleaded with him.

With Casey holding his hands and batting her eyelashes, what else could the guy do but agree?

The maid was ecstatic, the manager thrilled to have earned Casey's glowing smile. Adam found himself tipping the girl what he imagined would be half a week's wages. Which totally went against his policy of giving generously through organized charities. He suspected his sole motivation was to earn the same kind of approval from Casey that the manager had.

Why should I care what Casey thinks of me?

"See how easy that was?" she said, when they had the suite to themselves again. She beamed that wide smile he was coming to associate with her, an open smile that drew people to her with their problems and melted the hearts of hotel managers.

He wondered if it was a form of manipulation, and the thought provoked him. "What I see," he said, "is that you're as good at dealing out emotional blackmail as you are at taking it. You pressured that manager into something that's most likely against his job ethics."

When Casey put a hand to her mouth, stricken, he felt no satisfaction.

ADAM WOKE FROM AN UNEASY sleep on the couch in the middle of the night on Sunday. Make that Monday. The digital display on the clock across the room glowed 1:30 a.m.

He heard it again, the noise that must have woken him. A cry from upstairs.

Casey.

He pushed the sheet aside, rolled off the couch and grabbed his pants from the back of the chair. He hauled them on, then headed upstairs.

"Casey?" he called softly, noting she'd left the door ajar.

He snapped on the landing light and pushed the door open.

She lay sprawled in the center of the king-size bed, the duvet twisted across her lower body. Her top half was bare save for a strappy, satin confection in turquoise, which he guessed she'd chosen for her wedding night.

She didn't stir; whatever dream had disturbed her must have ended. Adam's mouth went dry and he felt like a voyeur. But, hell, how could any red-blooded man not notice Casey was gorgeous, even fully dressed? And Adam was as red-blooded as the next man. He also happened to be married to her.

Don't go there.

His marriage to Casey was strictly business. As they said on the infomercials: No Obligation, For a Limited Time Only. Of course, on those infomercials, they also said Satisfaction Guaranteed....

Damn. Adam pulled the door shut with a click that hopefully hadn't woken her, and went back to his couch.

And didn't sleep.

MONDAY, ADAM'S FAVORITE day of the week, found him overtired, overstressed and even more relieved than normal that the weekend had ended.

If he'd planned to fake a marriage to someone, he would have chosen someone tougher than Casey. Someone who could plow past other people's feelings in pursuit of her goal.

Not a woman who bought into the sob story of a hotel maid she'd never met before and then didn't hesitate to drag him into it, as well.

He wouldn't let her distract him from what he wanted to achieve in their month together, he told himself as he folded his clothes and packed his bag in preparation for their return to real life. He approached Casey, who had been packed and ready to go for ten minutes—he liked a woman who didn't keep him waiting—and said, "We need to set some ground rules."

"Hmm?" She looked up from her cross-stitching.

She'd taken a cross-stitch on her honeymoon. Adam wasn't sure if he admired her practicality or pitied her. Had she been sleeping with Joe so long that she wasn't anticipating any excitement?

He scowled at the thought of the intimacy she might have shared with her fiancé. "Ground rules," he said. "If we're living together for a month, we need some rules."

"You mean who gets to go first in the bathroom?" She smiled sunnily. "You go first. I don't have to get to work in the—"

"I have more than one bathroom," he interrupted, still trying to erase the idea of Casey in bed with that jerk. "I want to make sure we're in agreement about what's involved in this pretense. And what's not involved."

As if they didn't both know what was *not* involved. Casey kept her face blank, trying to appear undisturbed by what had hung heavy in the air between them all weekend. For goodness sake, they were virtually imprisoned in a honeymoon suite, with congratulatory cards and letters from complete strangers being delivered every half hour. Cards and letters addressed to Mr. and Mrs. Carmichael.

"For example," Adam said, "we're both free to spend our time as we wish. We don't owe each other any company."

"Sure," she agreed. "The last thing we'll want is to spend time together after we've been cooped up here so long." If that was true, how come she'd felt more alive this weekend than she had in years?

"But to convince our families our marriage is genuine, at times we'll have to exchange caresses and endearments." He sounded as if he was proposing some extreme form of torture.

"We seem to do okay on the caresses," she said, trying to be more positive than he was.

His brows drew together. "I like you, Casey, and I think we'll get along fine. But as soon as the annulment comes through, it's over. I wouldn't want you to think there's any chance of a permanent relationship between us."

Good grief, the guy had an ego. Just because she'd responded to his kisses like a heat-seeking missile locking on its target... Kisses that had sizzled in a way she'd never experienced with Joe...

"Ouch." She'd pierced her thumb with her needle. She sucked at the tiny hole, saw his eyes following her movement. She put down her needlework. "Adam," she said, "you're a good kisser, I'll grant you. But from what I've seen, you're single-minded about your work, you're resistant to change and you're emotionally unavailable. So don't *you* go getting any ideas, either." That was telling him.

"If emotionally unavailable means I don't want to adore anyone," he said, "you're damn right."

She wished she'd never mentioned "adoring" to him. It made her sound like a loser. She picked up her cross-stitching, squinted at the green thread she needed to knot. "I don't know why we're even talking about this," she said. "Sure, we'll be living in the same house for a month, but it's no big deal. You won't even know I'm there."

Adam watched her as she made some complicated maneuver with her needle. Watched his *wife*.

Through the glass tabletop he observed that her red skirt had ridden up to bare more thigh than he had any right to see. Her navy T-shirt hugged her curves, and she'd pulled her rich, honey-colored hair back into a loose ponytail that made her look like an eighteen-year-old.

A *hot* eighteen-year-old.

He sighed. He'd know she was there, all right.

THEY TOOK A TAXI from the Peabody to Adam's home in Germantown, an upmarket district about ten miles from downtown Memphis. Casey peered out her window as the cab drove through wrought-iron gates toward a three-story brick house. Make that a mansion. Yet the impressive pillared, Georgian-style structure had a welcoming look to it, enhanced by rolling green lawns and patches of colorful shrubbery.

She noted the high stone wall that edged one side of the property, and the thick hedge of poplars on the other. "I'll bet you never even see your neighbors," she said.

No one would be knocking on her door several times a day to borrow something or to ask if she could "mind the kids for an hour."

Adam looked alarmed. "No, I don't. And if I come home and find you've arranged a getting-to-know-you party or any such thing, this marriage will be over."

The taxi driver's eyes met Casey's in the rear-view mirror.

"No neighbors," she promised, putting a hand on her heart for effect. For the taxi driver's benefit, and to Adam's further alarm, she added, "Sweetheart."

Adam helped her out of the car while the driver retrieved their bags from the trunk. "I'll show you around before I head to the office."

She preceded him through the front door into a two-story lobby, breathing in the smell of beeswax from the gleaming oak parquet floor. Adam deposited their bags at the foot of the staircase and directed her into the living room.

Casey guessed the lobby and the living room between them were almost the size of her father's whole house in Parkvale. Having just escaped her long-time role of cook and cleaner, she shuddered.

Adam noticed. "Something wrong?"

She made a sweeping gesture that encompassed the Persian rugs, classic furniture and eclectic artwork. "This place is beautiful, but it must be a nightmare to clean. You might want to think about that next time you're looking for a wife. Any woman who took this on would have to be crazy. Or masochistic. Or…"

Too late she recognized the warning in his eyes and the signal in the barely discernible tilt of his head.

Casey turned and realized she'd come face-to-face with his housekeeper. A gray-haired, gray-faced woman in an apron regarded her with pursed lips and open disapproval.

"—or very well paid. Or a saint," Casey concluded, with an apologetic smile she hoped would redeem her. There was no answering smile. How dumb of her, not to have guessed Adam would have a housekeeper. She stuck out a hand to the woman, who took it reluctantly.

"I'm sorry," Casey said. "I didn't mean to insult you. The house looks wonderful. You obviously take pride in your work. I'm Casey Greene—Casey Carmichael."

"Selma Lowe," the woman said. "Pleased to meet you, Mrs. Carmichael."

A barefaced lie, if ever Casey had heard one. "Please, Selma, call me Casey."

Going by her sucking-a-lemon lips, Selma didn't take kindly to the suggestion.

"Thank you, Mrs. Lowe, that will be all," Adam said. "Don't go upsetting her," he warned Casey when the woman had gone. "She's worked here for years and I don't want to lose her. She's the most organized woman in Memphis."

"I've never upset anyone in my life." But it wasn't worth arguing the merits of nice over organized, Casey decided as she followed Adam upstairs.

He showed her to a guest bedroom with a

colonial-style king-size bed covered by a hand-stitched gray-and-white quilt. The window shutters had been flung open to let in the morning sunlight. Casey longed to slip out of her shoes and curl her toes into the plush navy-blue carpet.

"I hope you'll be comfortable," Adam said.

"It's lovely," she assured him. "Where's your room?"

He pointed to a door across the landing.

"Won't Selma—Mrs. Lowe—think it odd we're not sharing a room? Will she tell your stepmother?"

"Mrs. Lowe and Eloise despise each other. And Mrs. Lowe is the soul of discretion."

"If only you could have married her," Casey said brightly. More seriously, she added, "If she needs any help, or if you do, I'd be happy to—"

"That's exactly what I *don't* need," he said. "I don't need anything from you at all, beyond helping convince Eloise. My home life is very well organized. I don't want anything to change."

Once he was satisfied Casey knew her way around, he muttered something about going to work, and headed downstairs. Five minutes later, from her window, she saw a red Aston Martin DB9 sports car pass through the gates.

She only knew what sort of car it was because Joe had always held it up as his dream set of wheels. Imagine conservative order-freak Adam Carmichael owning one. If that wasn't sublimation of his teenage desire to race NASCAR, she would eat her Psychology 101 textbook.

Back downstairs, she found a less formal living room, where the morning newspaper lay neatly folded on a side table. She picked it up.

The headline jumped out at her: TV Couple's Peabody Love Nest. She groaned and began to read the article, which was just as sensational as the headline. According to the reporter, "Memphis's hottest couple, Adam and Casey Carmichael, spent the weekend closeted in their Romeo and Juliet Suite at the Peabody Hotel. They ordered in all their meals, including reputed aphrodisiacs champagne and oysters, say hotel staff, and unplugged the telephones. One employee described the Carmichaels as 'obviously very much in love.'"

Casey threw down the newspaper in disgust. "How much do they pay people to tell these lies?"

"Did you say something, Mrs. Carmichael?"

The silent approach of grim-faced Mrs. Lowe startled her, and Casey shrieked. The housekeeper bent to pick up the newspaper, and folded it back into shape with precise, sharp movements that Casey knew were designed to make her feel guilty.

But she didn't. In fact, she felt sorry for Mrs. Lowe. The poor woman must be worried that the new lady of the house would want to bring in her own staff. Casey wished she could tell the older woman to chill out, she'd be gone in a month. But

Adam hadn't said anything about dropping their pretense in front of the housekeeper.

"I'm planning country fried steak with gravy for dinner, Mrs. Carmichael."

"Really?" Casey managed to bite back her distaste. She didn't want to start off by disagreeing with Adam's perfect housekeeper, but surely it would be even more offensive when she didn't touch the fatty meal set before her tonight. "I don't know, Selma—Mrs. Lowe. It's such a hot day, do you think we could have something lighter? Maybe a chicken salad?"

"As you wish, Mrs. Carmichael." The woman glided from the room.

Whew, culinary crisis averted.

CHAPTER SIX

"WHERE'S MY COUNTRY FRIED steak? The gravy?"
Adam asked as Mrs. Lowe set a plateful of leafy
green stuff before him. Mrs. Lowe didn't reply but
as she left the room, her gaze flicked toward Casey.
He might have guessed.

Pretending he and Casey had a real marriage,
which in the confines of their suite at the Peabody
had seemed a brilliantly simple solution, now
seemed fraught with unexpected complexity. All
day at the office, when he should have been im-
mersed in his work, he'd found his thoughts drifting
to his honey-haired wife.

"Mrs. Lowe offered to prepare steak, but I asked
for a chicken salad instead," Casey said. "I don't
like a heavy meal on such a hot evening."

"But I had a light lunch today, knowing it was
my favorite for dinner." What hope did he have of
keeping her out of his thoughts, if he came home
every night to find his life disrupted? "I told you I
didn't want changes around here."

"I'm sorry, I won't interfere again."

His point made, Adam tackled the salad. It was delicious, as all Mrs. Lowe's meals were, and he started to feel better. He could always fill up on bread.

Prepared to be conciliatory, he said, "Are you missing out on your psychology classes, staying here?"

She shook her head. "Summer vacation. I start again in September."

"So what did you do today?"

Casey took a sip of her wine. "I read about you and me in the newspaper, saw the highlights of our wedding on the Channel Eight news and checked out which TV stations are showing *Kiss the Bride* this week—which are quite a few."

Adam made a mental note to tell the Channel Eight newsroom not to run any more stories about him and Casey. Then he remembered his strict policy of nonintervention in the news department. He sighed. "Did Eloise call?"

"The phone rang several times, but I wasn't sure if I should answer it. I think Mrs. Lowe took some messages."

"It's okay to answer it," he told her. "Did you do any work on your book?"

"I don't have it here with me," she said. "I have a couple of articles due to the newspaper I freelance for, too. I'll have to go back to Parkvale to fetch my files. Besides, I'll need more clothes. I thought I might take a bus home tomorrow, then I'll drive my car back here."

"A bus?" Adam thought about that as he chewed. "Why don't you do a one-way car rental? It'll be faster."

She hesitated, her fork halfway to her mouth. "I can't afford that. The bus will be fine."

"I'll pay for the rental."

Casey shook her head. "No thanks. Like you said, you don't want someone needy."

"I didn't mean it like that."

"I know, but I don't want to feel as if I'm taking advantage of you." She grinned. "What would Sam Magill say?"

"Forget Sam." Adam watched her evident enjoyment of her meal. "If my wife is seen taking a bus long distance, people will talk." He drummed his fingers on the table. This marriage was turning into a whole new set of obligations he didn't need. "I'll drive you to Parkvale myself. We'll leave early in the morning."

She opened her mouth, and he said, "Don't even think about offering to pay for the gas."

She closed it again.

He might as well get all his obligations out of the way. "There's one more thing." He reached into his pocket and pulled out a crimson velvet jeweler's box.

Casey bit her lip. Surely he hadn't gone out and bought her a ring?

He opened it and she saw a gold wedding band, engraved with a delicate, swirling pattern.

"This was my mother's," he said. "You'd better wear it while you're here."

"I don't think—"

"We're trying to make this marriage look real," he interrupted. "You have to wear it."

Casey extended her left hand. She could have sworn that, despite his impatience, Adam hesitated before he slid the gold band onto her finger.

His touch was warm as he held her hand for another moment, looking down at the ring. She couldn't help feeling that in wearing it she was joined to Adam by some invisible bond that hadn't been there a few minutes earlier.

"I guess your Mom's not around anymore," Casey said.

His expression became shuttered. "She died when I was ten years old. Just died in her sleep, no one knew why."

"How awful for you and your father."

Adam took his time finishing the last of his salad and she thought he wasn't going to answer. But he pushed his plate aside, looked her in the eye and said, "My father didn't give a damn. My mother loved him, but there was never a day in their life together when he acted as if he might love her back."

The raw pain in Adam's voice shocked Casey. "Did he love you?"

His black look said he resented the question, but maybe because he'd just put a ring on her finger, he answered it. "Dad loved the business."

She examined Adam's mother's ring, saddened that the woman who'd worn it before her had been unloved, at least by her husband. "You loved your Mom," she said to Adam.

"It wasn't enough," he said flatly. "She needed my dad, but it seemed he just didn't have it in him to love people. Like an illness that wasn't his fault."

Suddenly, Casey had an inkling about something. "What about Eloise?"

Adam scowled. "When he met Eloise he became a different person. He was crazy about her." His mouth tightened.

"You were jealous of Eloise?"

"I wasn't jealous, I was angry," he said calmly, but she could see a glint in his eyes. "Dad was so besotted with her, he lost all sense of balance. He lost focus at work—he'd take days off at a time to go away with her. He spent a fortune and let the business slide. Then I discovered—" He bit off his next words, pressed his lips together.

"But things came out right?" Casey asked.

Adam shrugged one shoulder uneasily. "When he woke up to how much trouble we were in, Dad did what he had to do. He mortgaged his house and poured money from his personal investments in to save the business and settle some of the lawsuits against the company. But he didn't want to tell Eloise. So she kept spending. Dad had a heart attack and died six months later." Adam paused, then delivered his damning judgment. "Because of Eloise, he lost control of the business he loved and paid for it with his life."

"Adam, I'm so sorry." Casey reached across the table and took his hand. Absently, he stroked the back of hers with his thumb, drawing a tingling energy to that spot.

"I've spent nearly seven years paying off the debts, getting back on top. It's been hard work, but they're all cleared. We're profitable, we're poised for major growth and we're finally starting to attract the bigger advertisers."

"You love that business as much as your father did," Casey observed. Suddenly, Adam's single-minded pursuit of what he wanted didn't seem selfish. It seemed like the only way he'd been able to get by.

He pulled his hand away. "I shouldn't have said anything—now your heart is going to bleed all over me. Forget it, Casey, it's all in the past."

"If you say so," she said doubtfully.

"Then stop frowning." He stroked a finger across her forehead.

"Frowning is your thing," she said. "Don't tell me we're already getting into that behave-alike married-couple thing."

Adam smiled reluctantly. "No chance of that."

CASEY FELL IN LOVE with the Aston Martin DB9 the moment Adam started the engine. Its quiet purr, the sensation of controlled power, its smooth acceleration to speeds she'd never traveled at before—it was bliss.

"This is wonderful, Adam. We'll be in Parkvale in an hour at this rate," she said in gross exaggeration as they sped northeast on I-40.

Adam eased off the gas a fraction. "It's a fast car," he agreed modestly.

They drove in silence for a while, but Casey found that when she was left alone with her thoughts, the air seemed to prickle with her awareness of Adam. To relieve the tension, she told him her theory about the Aston Martin as sublimation of his NASCAR ambitions. He snorted, but apparently didn't consider that worthy of comment.

"I don't suppose you want to drive my car back to Memphis and let me take this one?" she ventured some time later.

He started, as if she'd suggested an equal division of assets at the end of their month. "No one drives this car except me."

Casey sighed. "You NASCAR drivers are so selfish." That earned another snort.

Halfway there they stopped for gas. Relief propelled Adam out of the car. At last, a chance to put some distance between them. Didn't Casey realize the navy linen skirt, which looked so prim and proper, rode up her thighs every time she twisted to talk to him? A guy could crash his phenomenally expensive car with that kind of distraction.

Adam got back into the Aston Martin resolving to keep conversation—and thus thigh baring—to a minimum. But five minutes into the second half of the trip, it occurred to him he wasn't sure what to expect in Parkvale.

"Should I be worried about meeting your family?" he asked. "What are we going to say to them?"

Casey twisted in her red leather seat. Adam kept his gaze fixed on the road ahead.

"They won't be there," she said. "Karen's not due home until later in the week. And Tuesday morning is Dad's physical therapy. That's why I wanted to come today," she admitted. "I figured I'd sneak in and sneak out again."

"What about your brother?"

"Mike has a summer job in Dallas. But he's not as demanding as the other two—he's a typical young guy, caught up in his own stuff. It's Dad and Karen who are still calling me several times a day."

"We'll have to deal with them," Adam said. "They're going to want to meet your husband, so we should invite them to visit, maybe for a weekend."

"That's a great idea," she said. He knew without looking she'd be beaming again.

"The sooner you convince them you're truly out of their lives, the sooner I've kept my part of our bargain."

"I'll keep my part, too," she promised.

"I was going to talk to you about inviting Eloise over for dinner tomorrow night, so we can put on our happy couple act for her."

"That's what I'm here for," Casey agreed.

"Yep," he said. "I'm using you, you're using me. That's what this marriage is all about."

ALTHOUGH CASEY HAD NEVER said anything bad about her family, Adam had built up a mental image of her home as an environment of daily drudgery, enlivened only by her girlish dreams.

So he was surprised when they arrived in Parkvale and she directed him into the driveway of a freshly painted white cottage with a wisteria-draped porch.

Inside, the furnishings were simple, and obviously not expensive, but the place had been cheerfully and imaginatively decorated. Casey was, as he might have guessed, a good homemaker.

"It's nice," he said.

She gave him a knowing grin. "What did you expect?"

"I had no idea," he lied. "Did you do the decorating?"

She nodded. "I had a blitz in the spring. I thought the sight of me working might get Dad out of his armchair."

"Did it?"

"Bad call," she said, with a typical lack of resentment.

Upon closer observation, he realized everything was coated in a thin layer of dust. In the kitchen, dishes were piled in the sink and flies hovered over a mound of food scraps on the counter.

Casey headed toward the sink. "I might as well wash these."

"No, you won't." Adam moved quickly after her and clamped his hands on her shoulders. He turned her around, resisting the temptation to plant a kiss on the lips she'd parted in surprise. "Your father has to learn to cope without you, remember?"

"Yes, but—"

"Tough love," he reminded her. He released her to look at his watch. "I have a meeting at two o'clock. We need to get out of here." He was already looking forward to two and a half hours of peace and quiet, just him and the Aston Martin.

"You go ahead," Casey said. "I'll do a few things then follow in an hour or so."

"I'm not leaving you here to get sucked back into this family stuff. You've got a job to do back in Memphis." And when she looked blank, he added, "My stepmother, tomorrow night."

"You can't seriously think doing a few dishes is going to keep me here."

"It's not just the dishes," he said. "It's the egg baked onto the stovetop, the crumbs on the floor, the—"

Casey shuddered. "You're right, I can't believe I even thought about it." She walked briskly out of the kitchen. Over her shoulder, she said, "I'll get my things together. How about you back my car out? The key's on the hook in the kitchen."

Adam headed to the garage. "What the—"

Casey's blue Ford Fiesta might have been a peppy little car once, but not in the past twenty years. It was clean, but there were limits to how well rust scrubbed up. And while you could say the matching dents in both fenders lent it an air of symmetry, that was about all you could say.

"I didn't do those." Casey came into the garage with an armload of files. She stepped in front of one of the dents, as if to shield it from view. "They were both hit-and-runs in the hospital parking lot when I was visiting Dad."

"Dangerous places, hospitals," Adam said. He didn't ask why she was driving this heap of junk. He knew the answer. Money. So he wasn't about to wound her pride by suggesting they drop her car at a scrap dealer on the way out of town. "I'm following you back to Memphis."

Casey opened the back door and dumped the files on the seat. "Don't be so Neanderthal. This car is perfectly safe." She shut the door, but it didn't catch, so she opened it again and slammed it, which caused the window to drop to half-mast. She glared when Adam directed a pointed look at it. "You are *not* following me back."

"What are you going to do?" he taunted. "Outrun me?"

Her reply was drowned out by the sound of an engine, louder than a car's, in the driveway outside, followed by a screech of brakes, then a crash and the shattering of glass.

Adam had a horrible feeling he knew what that crash was. By the way Casey's face paled and how she edged away from him, she did, too.

Outside, doors closed with angry thuds.

"You idiot," a male voice yelled. "I drive all night to get you here. All I ask is that you take over for the last half hour so I can sleep, and this is what happens."

"You might have told me this damn truck takes ten minutes to stop after you press the brake," a female voice accused. "What is that…that *thing,* anyway? Who put it there?"

Adam pressed the button next to the light switch and the garage door opened. He stepped forward into the sunlight. "I did. And it's an Aston Martin DB9."

At least, that's what it used to be. Now it was an Aston Martin DB9 with built-in U-Haul. Adam winced at the sight of the truck wrapped around his bumper.

The woman, who turned out to be a younger, not-so-pretty version of Casey, yelped.

Casey ran forward. "Karen, it's me." She hugged her sister, and Karen stuck to her like a prickly bur. Casey shook her, but didn't manage to detach her. "Where's the baby? Karen, is Rosie with you?"

"She's with her father. He's going to bring her down this weekend." Karen hiccupped on a sob. "You came home," she said. "I knew you would. Oh, Casey, thank you, *thank you*." She squeezed her tighter, then said tremulously, "Is this…is this your rental car I smashed? I'm sorry. I didn't expect anything to be in the driveway. But I'll pay for it, I promise." She directed a doubtful look at the Aston Martin—even in its current state, it looked like a million dollars. "Uh, did you take the insurance option on the rental?"

Adam met Casey's eyes over her sister's head, which she was patting reassuringly. She gave him a breezy smile, one that said, *I have this under control.* It didn't fool him. He counted to five, long enough to convince himself the damage to his car wouldn't get any worse if he waited a few minutes to inspect it.

"It's my car," he said, "I'm Adam Carmichael." She lifted her head, looked at him blankly. He didn't want to say it, but it was somehow easier than saying he was Casey's husband. "Your brother-in-law."

She frowned. "What are you doing here?"

"Karen!" Casey turned to Adam. "She's in shock from the accident, she's not usually—"

"Such a pain," interjected the still visibly simmering young man who'd been standing to one side. "Yes, she is, Casey, and you know it."

That set Karen crying again. Casey glared at him. "Adam, this is Mike. My brother. Who can be equally painful when he chooses."

Mike grinned and maneuvered around Karen to give Casey a belated kiss on the cheek. Then he shook hands with Adam. "Sorry about your car. That's one hot set of wheels. Automatic or stick shift?"

"Stick shift." Adam forced a smile.

"It's great to see you, Mike," Casey said.

Taking her cue from her sister, Karen said, "Mike's been wonderful. He loaded this thing for me—" she indicated the U-Haul "—then he drove through the night. I couldn't have done it without him." She wrapped her arms around her brother.

Adam suppressed a shudder. Karen was a clinging vine.

"Did Dad tell you I was coming today?" Karen asked. "It's so cool you're here to help."

Adam could see alarm in Casey's eyes. They hadn't survived a wedding and a honeymoon for her to give in now.

"My wife and I—" that turned out to be easier to say than he expected "—are due back in Memphis right away."

Karen looked around as if she was trying to figure out who Adam's wife was.

"So Casey and I," Adam clarified, "can't help you."

Casey shifted from one foot to the other. "Adam, that's a little harsh. I can stay a few hours."

He mouthed something at her, and Casey recognized the words *tough love*. She bit her lip. He was right. Postponing by two or three hours what Karen would see as her abandonment wouldn't change anything.

She cleared her throat. "We're not staying, Karen." She stepped closer to Adam. He locked her hand in his, and she sent him a startled glance. That's right, they were pretending this marriage was genuine.

Tears filled Karen's eyes again.

Adam tightened his grip on Casey's hand and eyeballed Mike.

"Casey has to go," Mike told Karen. "I'll help you unload." Adam continued to stare at him, until the younger man said, "I'll stay on a couple of days until you're settled."

Karen nodded, dragged her sleeve across her eyes in a curiously childish gesture. "I—I love you, Casey."

How the hell was Adam supposed to compete with that? Karen must know it was exactly what her sister wanted to hear. He couldn't tighten his grip on Casey any more without hurting her. He settled for caressing the finger that bore his mother's wedding ring.

"I love you, too, sweetie," Casey said. "Too much to stay."

She was shaking as she turned away from Karen. Adam wrapped an arm around her, shepherded her to inspect the damage to his car. It wasn't too bad—drivable despite broken taillights and a dented bumper. At his request, Mike moved the U-Haul onto the lawn to clear the driveway.

"Go pack some clothes," Adam told Casey. "I'll get the Aston Martin out of the way, then I'll move that thing you call a car out of the garage."

The Fiesta started first try, which was something. Adam drove it outside, moved the driver's seat back to where he thought Casey had had it, then got out. When he walked around the back of the Fiesta, he got an eyeful of the sticker fixed to the back bumper.

Honk If You Think I'm Sexy.

He was still trying to convince himself it couldn't really say anything so tacky, when Casey emerged from the house lugging a suitcase and a carry-all that was almost bursting at the seams.

"What is *this?*" He pointed at the offending sticker. "Let me guess, it's affirming?"

Her smile, shaky after the encounter with Karen, told him he'd got it in one.

"It was Brodie-Ann's idea," she said. "And I must admit, it works."

He rolled his eyes. "I'll bet it does. Brodie-Ann has a lot to answer for. Are you ready?"

"Yep. I left a note for Dad to say I'll call him about getting us all together."

Adam stowed Casey's bags in the Fiesta's trunk while she detached herself from a prolonged good-bye hug with Karen. He waited until she was out of the driveway before he headed for his own car.

Casey drove off at a speed that could charitably be called sedate. More like a snail's pace. Adam sighed as he turned his key in the ignition of the Aston Martin. This would be a long trip.

He pulled out his cell phone; he needed to call his secretary and cancel his two-o'clock meeting, then phone his insurance company. At this speed, driving one-handed presented no problems.

Within three blocks, the honking started.

CHAPTER SEVEN

ADAM'S BRIEF HAD BEEN simple. His stepmother would come for dinner. Adam and Casey would act loving, which according to him meant he would call her darling and hold her hand. They'd have an excellent meal, served by the efficient Mrs. Lowe, then Eloise would go home, fully deluded that her stepson had done what she wanted and married a woman he loved. And the logical outcome was that she would stay out of Adam's life. No more party planning, no more introductions to eligible women, no more bridefest.

"How will she feel when we get an annulment?" Casey had asked.

"She'll get over it."

"Adam!" His callousness shocked Casey.

"What?"

She narrowed her eyes, and he threw up his hands. "All right, she might be disappointed at first. But by then I'll have a plan in place for dealing with Aunt Anna May's lawsuit, the business will be secure and Eloise will see it's all good."

The finality of it silenced Casey. "If you're sure," she said at last.

"Quite sure. I know my stepmother. Don't worry, this plan is perfect."

OH, YEAH?

Adam had reckoned without his wife's ability to disrupt his arrangements, Casey thought grimly, as Mrs. Lowe, back ramrod straight, stalked out the front door and climbed into a waiting taxi.

How had this happened? All Casey had done was offer to make dessert, and the housekeeper had taken off her apron and said with chilly politeness, "Mrs. Carmichael, I am not used to having my work questioned. You may no longer require my services, but many other people do. I will leave now, and I will telephone Mr. Carmichael to send on my wages."

Ten minutes later, she was gone.

The kitchen clock showed quarter to six. Casey's new mother-in-law—or was she a stepmother-in-law?—was due in fifteen minutes, and right now dinner comprised a half-assembled hors d'oeuvres tray, several piles of chopped vegetables and a bowl of marinating meat.

This was all Adam's fault, she thought crossly. He'd promised to be home by five-thirty. If he'd been on time, he could have cajoled Mrs. Lowe into staying.

Reluctantly, Casey decided to phone him and confess. It would mean facing his anger sooner rather than later, but at least he could call Eloise and ask her to postpone. By tomorrow, Casey could whip up a decent meal.

She dialed his cell phone on the assumption he was on his way home. When he answered, the tension in his voice made her hesitate to give him the bad news.

"I'm glad you called, Casey. I'm afraid I'm going to be late, so you'll have to look after Eloise for a while. I wouldn't ask, but it's an emergency." She heard agitated voices behind him, and Adam lowered his tone to murmur, "I'm in a room full of lawyers, trying to figure out how not to lose several million dollars." He paused. "Did you want something?"

"Uh, no, nothing important. I'll see you later." Casey hung up the phone. She briefly considered ordering pizza, but if Eloise was a stickler for routine like her stepson, that would be a very bad idea.

She looked at the dinner ingredients on the counter. Steak, mushrooms, potatoes, salad, garlic, strawberries… She could do something with these.

CASEY HAD EXPECTED Adam's stepmother to display the same unshakeable love of order as he did, and arrive right on time. But fortunately, the doorbell didn't chime until twenty past six. Casey went to the front door, only remembering as she opened it that she was still wearing Mrs. Lowe's voluminous apron.

The tall, elegant, silk-clad woman on the door-step had light-blue eyes that right now were coolly assessing.

"Mrs. Carmichael?" Casey said brightly. "I'm Casey."

"Well." Eloise sounded bemused rather than hostile. "You look rather different from when I saw you on television on Friday." Then, as Casey hesitated, she asked, "Are you going to invite me in?"

"I'm working in the kitchen," Casey explained as she followed her mother-in-law across the foyer. When Eloise looked around, bewildered, Casey wondered if she even knew where Adam's kitchen was. She led the way, aware of the silent tread of her bare feet in contrast to the clack of Eloise's heels on the parquet floor.

"Where's Mrs. Lowe?" Eloise surveyed the clutter on the counter, sniffed the baking shortcake. She cast a wary glance around.

"I'm afraid she's gone," Casey said. "I said something to offend her—again—and she walked out."

Eloise broke into a huge smile that stripped away the suspicion, the cool elegance, and left her looking like someone's mother. "Bravo, my dear," she said. "If I'd known it was that easy, I'd have tried it years ago. This calls for a drink."

She got a bottle of champagne from the refrigerator, but clearly had no idea how to open it. Casey did the honors. Eloise raised a glass of the fizzing liquid.

"Good riddance to Mrs. Lowe," she said.

Casey joined her in the toast, feeling rather disloyal to Adam, but sharing the sentiment wholeheartedly.

"So," Eloise said, "have you told Adam yet?" Her eyes gleamed with anticipation.

"I called, but it wasn't a good time. He's running late, by the way, and sends his apologies. Mrs. Carmichael, do you think—"

"My dear Casey, you can't call me Mrs. Carmichael," she said in her soft Southern drawl. "You may call me Mother—" she saw the doubt on Casey's face "—or Eloise, if you prefer."

"Eloise, then." Casey looked around the kitchen, a trifle wildly. "Adam's having a really bad day at work. Yesterday his car got smashed thanks to me—" Eloise drew in a sharp breath that acknowledged the importance of the Aston Martin "—and now I've lost his precious housekeeper. Maybe I should tell him tomorrow, let him think Mrs. Lowe cooked tonight."

Eloise tilted her elegantly coiffed head to one side. "Not a chance. That old dragon never makes strawberry shortcake. She knows it's my favorite. It won't take Adam two minutes to notice something's wrong."

Casey had feared as much. She groaned and got

back to her dinner preparations. To her surprise, Eloise pitched in and helped, with a lot of enthusiasm if not much actual skill. Adam's tale about his father had given Casey the impression Eloise might be demanding or selfish, but right now she was neither.

By the time Adam arrived home a half hour later, the steak had been seared and was ready to be finished off in the oven, the mushroom sauce was made, the vegetables were awaiting a final steaming, and the hors d'oeuvres tray was a fully assembled work of art.

When they heard the front door open, Casey and Eloise froze, as if they'd been caught stealing the silver.

"You run upstairs and change," Eloise said. "I'll head Adam off at the pass." She chortled as she snatched up the champagne bottle and headed out to the foyer.

"Adam, darling…" Her voice wafted back to the kitchen.

As Casey raced up the back staircase, she heard her cooing at her stepson, and getting what sounded like a grunt in response. It didn't seem as if Adam's day had improved any. Casey grimaced at her reflection in her bedroom mirror. She was flushed with heat—and, no doubt, with champagne. Grease streaked her face and her hair hung limply. Too bad she didn't have time for a shower.

She splashed cold water over her face and upper body, then twisted her hair and pinned it at the back of her head. Thankful she'd had the forethought to select her clothes earlier, she put on the silky lilac dress, taking pleasure in the way it shimmied over her hips. The slim fit showed her figure off to advantage, and a slit up the side enabled freedom of movement. Quickly, she applied lipstick—no need for blusher. She grimaced as she realized a few tendrils of hair had already escaped their pins.

On her way to join the others, she collected the hors d'oeuvres from the kitchen. The heavy tray forced her to slow her pace, so she had a moment to collect herself.

When Casey entered the living room, Adam moved immediately to relieve her of it. Although she was expecting some kind of embrace, she flinched when his lips touched her forehead.

"Darling," he said, as he set the hors d'oeuvres down on the table, "you should let Mrs. Lowe do this."

Casey looked at Eloise, who frowned and tipped her head toward Adam's untouched champagne glass. Eloise was right. It might be better for him to relax with a drink before Casey gave him the bad news. "It was no problem…honey," she said.

"But Mrs. Lowe—" Adam began.

Casey did the only thing she could think of to forestall the inevitable. She stood on tiptoe and planted a firm kiss on his mouth. Time slowed as she absorbed the sureness of his lips against hers. Her hands went to his chest to brace herself, and she felt the strength of his muscles beneath the crisp cotton of his shirt. The kiss lasted barely two seconds, but when she pulled away, Casey felt herself blushing furiously.

"What was that for?" Adam sounded dazed— and not at all like he was thinking about his house- keeper.

"You had a bad day. I wanted to make it better." She took a step backward. "Did it work?"

He touched a finger to his lips. "Well, it didn't hurt any."

"How did your meeting go with the lawyers?" Casey asked.

"It, uh, wasn't too bad," he said distractedly.

"Adam, I must congratulate you on your wife," Eloise said. "She's lovely." She smiled at Casey.

Adam didn't look at Casey, but took her hand, entwined his fingers loosely with hers. "Yes, she is."

Eloise lifted her glass in a toast. "To true love, the kind that lasts forever."

Casey raised her glass with only the tiniest twinge of guilt. She still believed in true love, even if it didn't have a place in her marriage. Adam muttered something about forever being a very long time, but at last he drank some champagne. By the time they finished the hors d'oeuvres, he'd had two glasses and did seem more relaxed, though Casey could still see that furrow in his brow.

"I'll go check on things in the kitchen," she said. "Why don't you two go through to the dining room?"

She steamed the vegetables and reheated the sauce while the meat finished cooking in the oven. She served the meal with some pride—she'd done a great job at short notice.

When she carried all three plates into the dining room—a skill she'd acquired waiting tables to help pay her father's medical bills—the atmosphere was like thunder. Adam was glowering at his step-mother, who looked decidedly sheepish.

"What's going on?" Casey asked.

"Eloise has confessed that she annoyed Mrs. Lowe so much tonight, the poor woman quit," Adam said.

Something seized in Casey's chest. She set the plates down carefully. "Eloise, that is the nicest thing you could have done." She blinked and clamped her lips together to stop the prickle behind her eyes from turning into an overflow of emotion. When she was sure she could continue, she said, "Adam, it was my fault." Briefly, she recounted the true sequence of events.

"I figured I can do the cooking and look after the house for the next…while," she finished.

Adam had the same black look he'd worn the night Casey had canceled the country fried steak. Only this situation wouldn't be so easily resolved.

"Darling, don't be silly." He smiled, but he spoke through gritted teeth. His doting husband act required him to stifle his annoyance in front of Eloise. "This house is so big, no self-respecting wife would take it on. I'll call the agency and find a replacement."

"Perhaps Casey should interview the candidates," Eloise suggested, "to make sure she finds someone she likes."

Adam agreed. Even if his acquiescence was just for Eloise's benefit, Casey decided she would contact the agency in the morning. It was the least she could do.

Over dinner, Eloise demanded details of their romance—where they'd met and how long they'd known each other.

"Here in Memphis and long enough." Adam's evasive reply covered both questions.

He stopped just short of being rude to Eloise. He might claim any ill-feeling toward his stepmother was in the past, but obviously he still held a grudge.

"You must be a very special woman, Casey," she said. "I think Adam always believed he couldn't have both the business and a woman he loved, and he was far more comfortable with the business."

Adam scowled. "Eloise knows nothing about it," he said.

His stepmother ignored that. "I'm sure he's figured out by now that a marriage built on true love will strengthen him, rather than weaken him."

Adam clutched his head in his hands. "Spare me two amateur psychologists in the family."

Later, when Eloise rose to leave, she hugged Casey warmly. "I can't wait to get to know you better, my dear." To Adam, she said, "I know you'll be relieved not to have me foisting young women on you every time I see you."

"You bet," he answered, with more enthusiasm than he'd displayed toward her all night.

TOO EASY.

By Friday, Casey had recruited a new housekeeper, Adam having failed in his attempt to persuade Mrs. Lowe to return. Sue Mason was good-natured, young enough to be happy about using first names, and keen to start work on Monday. Those were all the qualifications she needed as far as Casey was concerned. She'd asked Adam his opinion, and he'd told her to go ahead and do what she thought best. He probably planned to find a carbon copy of Mrs. Lowe as soon as the annulment came through.

But for now, Casey thought, as she put the phone down after confirming Sue's employment, everything was going just fine. She and Adam had been married for a week, and she'd already made good progress on her book. Karen was still calling several times a day for advice about Rosie, but Casey's ignorance on the subject of babies meant she couldn't be of more than limited help. By the time their one-month marriage was over, Casey and Adam should both have achieved their goals.

Who needs to be adored?

THE SECOND WEEK of their marriage flew by. Everything was running smoothly in the house, thanks to the new housekeeper. Adam was busy at work, and Casey's days involved plenty more writing, punctuated by visits from Eloise, who seemed determined to get to know her daughter-in-law. When Casey mentioned to Adam she felt guilty about deceiving Eloise, he gave her a lecture about focus and selfishness.

The next Sunday, they had lunch at the Peabody Hotel with Eloise and two of her friends, Celeste and Beth. Adam told Casey that whenever his stepmother was home, he took the ladies to Sunday lunch. "It lets me off the hook of having to see her the rest of the week," he explained.

But it seemed to Casey the way her husband treated Eloise and her companions went beyond routine courtesy. He made considerable effort to charm the three women he called the Merry Widows, as they sat at the best table in the house. The Peabody staff had greeted Casey and Adam like long-lost friends.

Casey sipped on her mint julep tea, ordered at Eloise's urging and served in a tall frosted glass.

The refreshing combination of bourbon, mint and tea should have helped her relax. But Eloise had introduced her to the other ladies as "my dear daughter-in-law," and Casey found herself the center of the conversation. She felt like a fraud.

When Adam waved at someone, she was ready to welcome any distraction. Even Sam Magill, the lawyer, who'd arrived with another group. Sam caught Adam's signal and excused himself from his friends.

"What is that man doing here?" Eloise creased the fine linen napkin between her fingers as she watched him approach. How did he do this, turn up wherever she went? She couldn't so much as take Adam a tray of his favorite cornbread at the office without Sam popping up to ask if she'd taken her blood pressure medication, or to remind her it was time to pay her federal taxes, or to warn her a prowler had been sighted in her area. Now he was fiddling with his tie, which was already perfectly knotted, and in his distraction he bumped an elderly woman's chair on his way over.

Sam stopped to check if the old lady was all right, then at last reached their table.

"Eloise." He greeted her with a half bow, just as James used to. When James did it, she'd thought it charming.

"Hello, Sam."

Sam knocked her purse, which she'd hung over

the back of her chair. He apologized, red in the face. Feeling sorry for him, Eloise smiled. Hope leaped into his eyes. Oh, dear. Sam could interpret even ordinary courtesy as something more when he wanted to badly enough.

That visit she'd paid to his house had revealed he cared for her more deeply than she'd suspected. It wasn't fair to let it continue. Somewhere out there was a woman who would return his feelings.

Eloise bit her lip. Though it went against her upbringing, though her mama would have a fainting fit if she were alive to witness it, maybe Eloise should be…less polite to Sam.

For both their sakes.

She turned her back on him to speak to Celeste, making the exclusion deliberate.

Sam's voice was gruff when he said to Adam, "I planned to call you at home this afternoon."

It was rare for Sam to phone on the weekend. Adam figured it couldn't be good news. He reached around to the empty table behind him and pulled a chair over for Sam. "What's the problem?"

The attorney directed an anxious glance at Eloise as he sat down, but she wasn't paying him any attention. "I heard a rumor from the offices of your aunt's lawyer. Your marriage—" he nodded to Casey, sitting next to Adam "—has Anna May worried you've met the conditions of the will and put Henry out of contention."

"That figures," Adam said.

"So she's claiming," the lawyer said, "your father was out of his mind when he wrote that will."

Adam gripped the edge of the table. If Anna May and Henry were here, he'd knock their stupid heads together. This time, they'd gone too far.

"My father was *not* crazy." His anger erupted at the worst possible moment. The waiter had arrived with their food, and the women had stopped talking. Everyone at Adam's table heard his declaration. And judging by the curious glances directed their way, everyone at neighboring tables, too.

"Adam?" Eloise said uncertainly.

This news would hurt his stepmother. He wished he didn't care, but… Casey reached over to prize his fingers from the table edge. She curled her hand around his and squeezed gently.

Adam felt the tension seep out of him. Whatever Anna May was up to, they would get past it.

"It's Anna May's latest tactic," he told his stepmother. "She's claiming Dad wasn't of sound mind when he wrote his will."

He was about to add that his aunt wouldn't get anywhere with such a preposterous claim, when Sam blurted, "She has evidence."

Eloise uttered a word Adam didn't know she knew, not quite under her breath. Sam coughed into his handkerchief.

"Are you still smoking, Mr. Magill?" Eloise gave

the lawyer a chilly look that cleared his cough miraculously. "Such a bad habit," she said to no one in particular. "James smoked cigars when I met him, but he stopped eventually. He always felt it bespoke a lack of self-control."

Sam made a choking noise.

Casey blinked. She'd never heard Eloise be anything less than charming.

"But then," her mother-in-law continued, "what would James have known about it? Given he was *insane.*" She spoke lightly, but fixed Sam with a gimlet glare.

The lawyer blushed, and Casey felt sorry for him. From the second he'd approached their table, it had been obvious he had a crush on Eloise. His harshedged self-assurance evaporated, and it seemed all he could do was open his mouth and insert both feet.

"I didn't say James was insane," Sam mumbled. From somewhere, he dredged up a speck of his usual confidence. "I had a lot of respect for James, Eloise. You know that."

She nodded jerkily. But when she spoke, she still sounded hostile. "Then you won't let Anna May get away with this, will you?"

Sam looked as if he badly wanted to assure her that hell would freeze over before Anna May got to say anything against James in open court. But from the way he squirmed in his seat, Casey guessed the answer wasn't that straightforward.

"I believe Anna May has a sworn statement with regard to your husband's state of mind. That statement is the basis of her case," the lawyer said formally.

Eloise gave a decidedly unladylike snort. "I'll bet she has no such thing."

"Who made the statement?" Casey asked.

The lawyer's eyes widened, as if he hadn't anticipated what was surely an obvious question. Yet more evidence he didn't think straight when Eloise was around. He shot a pleading look at Adam. "We should continue this discussion tomorrow."

"We want to know now," Eloise said.

Adam nodded at Sam to continue. The attorney closed his eyes as if in pain. "The statement is from one of the nonfamily directors of Carmichael Broadcasting. He had a conversation with another director, in which that director expressed a firm opinion that James Carmichael had lost his mind."

"Which other director?" Adam and Eloise demanded simultaneously.

Sam slumped in his seat and raised his hands, conceding defeat to the forces ranged against him. "It was you, Adam."

CHAPTER EIGHT

As Casey and Eloise stared at Adam, a flash of white light blinded them.

"Thanks, folks." A photographer, a man Casey recognized from the crowd who'd gathered at the TV studio after their wedding, slipped his camera back into its case. "Enjoy your meal."

Lunch pretty much fell apart after that.

Adam began to deny the accusation, then he went beet-red and clammed up.

Eloise's eyes filled with hurt. She stood up. "I can ignore Anna May's poison—that woman's always been a fool. But, Adam, for you to say such a thing about your father, a man who, whatever you may think, loved you. The finest, most intelligent man I've known…" She stopped, and Casey saw her throat working with emotion. "*That* is a betrayal." She slipped her purse off the back of her chair, then asked a passing waiter to bring her coat. "Thank you for lunch," she said with her usual good manners, "but I plan to take a taxi home."

The other two Merry Widows glared at Adam—extending their hostility to encompass Casey by association—with a ferocity that made Casey hope neither of them was packing a weapon.

Sam sprang to his feet. "Eloise, how can I help you? You shouldn't be alone if you're upset. I can take you—"

Eloise gave him a look that said he'd done enough, and stalked out of the restaurant.

Celeste and Beth left with her, while Adam settled the bill. Casey followed him outside, where the valet reluctantly relinquished the newly repaired Aston Martin.

Adam pulled out into the traffic with a screech of tires. From the passenger seat, Casey cast him a sidelong glance. A frown darkened his face, and his chin jutted forward.

"What?" he demanded.

She spread her hands. "I didn't say anything."

"You didn't have to," he grumbled. "I can see you think I'm a prize jerk."

"You're certainly a contender," she agreed. "But right now I'm giving you the benefit of the doubt."

He managed a half smile. "Thanks, but it's more than I deserve. I did tell John Hanson I thought Dad had lost his marbles. Years ago, a few months before the heart attack."

The self-recrimination in his eyes gave Casey the urge to comfort her husband, to wrap her arms around him and tell him it would be all right. Instead, she said, "Did you mean it?"

Adam shook his head, then nodded. "In a heat-of-the-moment way. I'd just found out Carmichael Broadcasting's accountant had been embezzling funds. It seemed Dad had lost touch with reality when he married Eloise. The business was on the brink of disaster, and I vented to John Hanson. Big mistake."

"No judge will accept a one-off remark as evidence your father was insane," Casey said.

Adam grimaced. "There was one other occasion. At the reading of Dad's will, when I heard about that marriage clause, I did say something along the lines of, 'He must have been nuts.' Eloise didn't take it well at the time. Anna May was there, too. I'm sure she'll remember."

"But still," Casey persisted, "it's not exactly expert psychiatric testimony."

"Which we can't get, now that Dad's dead," he pointed out. "Maybe what I said isn't enough. But maybe we'll get a judge who agrees that what Dad did was crazy, and he'll order a full hearing."

Adam stopped at a red light. To think his own careless remark had fueled Anna May's case. His foot tapped the brake.

"You made a mistake," Casey said. "But you'll get past it."

He turned to face her, found her expression full

of sympathy. Casey was on his side, without reservation. She reached across to squeeze his hand on the steering wheel—only it felt more as if she'd squeezed all the air out of his lungs. She snatched her hand back, but not before Adam had seen the flare of desire in her eyes—one that matched his own.

"It might hurt Eloise less if you call to apologize," she said.

Damn if she hadn't tapped into the vein of guilt he tried to pretend didn't exist. Adam didn't need this. "What are you, my wife?"

She snickered, her cheek dimpling, and Adam found himself saying, "I'll think about it."

IT WAS UNUSUAL for Brodie-Ann to take a day off work just so she could drive up to Memphis and have lunch with Casey.

When Casey got to the downtown bistro where they'd agreed to meet on Tuesday, the woman who would spill the contents of her soul at the slightest urging shied away from Casey's questions, deflecting the conversation at their courtyard table to news of what was going on in Parkvale.

"I saw your sister out with the baby last week," Brodie-Ann said.

"How were they?" Casey asked over a lump in her throat. She missed her family, even if she didn't want to be back with them.

"We chatted for a few minutes, then Karen got teary."

Casey chewed her lip. "Maybe I should call her tonight."

"She didn't seem too bad," Brodie-Ann assured her. "It might have just been new-mom hormones."

It wasn't until the waiter had set their chicken Caesars in front of them that Brodie-Ann got to what might have been the point of this get-together.

"Is marriage what you expected?" she asked.

Casey took a sip of her ice water. "I can't say I ever thought about what it might be like to be married to a complete stranger who happens to be the cutest guy I ever met, even if he is a little set in his ways." She put her glass down and turned the question back on Brodie-Ann. "Is marriage what *you* expected?"

Her friend ducked the issue. "So you think Adam's cute, huh?"

Was Brodie-Ann blind? Could she not see he was *gorgeous?* Casey bit back the suggestion that her friend have her eyes tested. "Sure I do. He's a great guy, too." No point denying it.

"Does he have you ironing his shirts yet? Taking meals to his dying grandmother? Hosting soirees for important clients?"

Casey shook her head. "None of the above. He doesn't need me at all." Somehow that came out sounding pathetic.

"That's great," Brodie-Ann said uncertainly. "I'll bet you're enjoying the break."

"Absolutely." Then why did Casey suddenly feel lost?

Brodie-Ann glanced at her watch, then said with a strange urgency, "Casey, sweetie, does Adam like you back?"

"I don't think so." Why would he want a woman who had nothing to offer him? *This is stupid. For years I've wanted to get away from people who only want me for what I can do for them.* What was she, a dependence junkie? "Like I told you," she said, "we're sticking together until the annulment comes through, that's all."

When the waiter appeared suddenly to top up their water glasses, her friend jumped a mile high.

"What's the matter with you?" Casey demanded. "I've never seen you so on edge."

Brodie-Ann flicked a glance over her shoulder across the crowded courtyard. "Nothing. I thought it was…" She stopped, nibbled on a thumbnail.

"You're scaring me," Casey said. "I know you didn't come here for a chat, so tell me what's going on with you and Steve. Right now."

To her shock, Brodie-Ann put her hands over her face, and her shoulders started to shake. Casey dropped her fork and moved around the table to hug her friend. "Honey, what's wrong?"

Brodie-Ann pulled herself together and wriggled

out of Casey's embrace. "I'm sorry, I'm being silly." She waved Casey back to her seat and managed a watery smile. "It's just…it's not how I thought it would be. I mean, I still adore Steve, but it's not…" She gulped, on the verge of crying again.

"What's he done? Is he mean to you?" Casey half rose from her chair again.

Brodie-Ann laughed. "Can you imagine Steve being mean to anyone? He's wonderful. I'm lucky to have him."

"But?" Casey prompted.

"You'll think I'm so selfish." Brodie-Ann's gaze slid away from hers. "Before we were married, Steve was so romantic, he'd do anything for me. Once, he even laid his coat down in a puddle so I could step across, just like that guy did for Queen Elizabeth."

Casey looked suitably impressed, though she wouldn't dream of stepping on a man's coat, even if he did lay it down for her—she'd only have to launder it afterward. That kind of romantic gesture was all very well, but the kind of guy Casey could love would be one who…

Who drops my cell phone into a vase when he sees the caller is upsetting me.

Who listens when I suggest he apologize to his stepmother, then goes and does it. And thanks me afterward.

Who from the very start of our marriage has made my goals as much a priority as his.

Casey clapped a hand over her mouth, as if her thoughts might escape.

I am not falling for Adam Carmichael.

"Did you even hear what I said?" Brodie-Ann demanded.

Casey shook her head in mute apology.

Her friend tutted. "Steve still does those things sometimes, but often as not, I'm the one who's making sacrifices. And it's all bigger stuff than walking on coats. It's giving up my time, my priorities."

"Does he give up those things, too?"

Brodie-Ann nodded glumly. "But he was always good like that. I'm not. I've always been about, well, about *me*," she said with such honesty that Casey laughed. "I'm horrible, aren't I?" she said plaintively. "As soon as Steve figures that out, he'll leave me."

"Steve fell in love with the real you," Casey reminded her. "Yes, you can be demanding. But he loves that. You can also be sweet and generous. He loves that, too. I'm right, aren't I?"

Brodie-Ann didn't reply. But though her lips curved in only the smallest of smiles, her eyes gleamed. Casey fought a twinge of envy.

"Honey, these things take time," she said. "You and Steve are made for each other, but that doesn't mean you don't have to work at your marriage. That's a good thing."

"I guess." Her tone wasn't enthusiastic, but Brodie-

Ann looked happier. Then she started chewing her thumbnail again. "Casey, I have a confession."

Casey realized the flush on her friend's face was guilt. "What have you done?"

"While I was worrying about whether I was right to marry Steve, I started to think about you and Joe. And although the wedding didn't work out, I wondered if maybe *you* were right that you should marry someone you know really well." Brodie-Ann babbled on, getting pinker by the second. "Obviously, I didn't know that you, uh, liked Adam, so when Joe came to see me last night and asked if he thought he had any chance of getting back with you, and I was having lunch with you today, I, um…"

A shadow fell across the table, and she stopped.

"Hello, Casey," Joe said.

Her ex-fiancé stood there, handsome in his navy uniform, twisting his cap in his hands.

"Sorry," Brodie-Ann murmured. She pushed her chair back. "I'll let you guys talk." Before Casey could grab her, she was gone, crossing the courtyard at a pace just short of a run.

"May I?" Joe sat in Brodie-Ann's chair without waiting for an answer.

A clammy heat dampened Casey's palms, gave her itchy feet. She'd been fine talking to Brodie-Ann about Parkvale, but now, seeing Joe, she felt her old life reaching out to her with long, bony fingers. She wanted to shrink away from him and sprint after her friend.

"I should have called you." Joe read the reluctance in her face. "But after what I did, I wasn't sure you'd talk to me. I had to tell you how sorry I am."

An apology? That's why he was here? Not to get back together with her? The threat receded, and Casey's relief came out as a shaky laugh. "Don't worry about it," she said. "I shouldn't have tricked you into going to the TV studio. It was humiliating for both of us." She smiled wryly. "Although you might have told me sooner that you didn't love me."

Joe grabbed her hand across the table, leaning forward so his eyes gazed directly into hers.

"It wasn't true. You've always been my girl, Casey, since we were eighteen years old." Urgency raised the pitch of his voice. "I panicked, I made a mistake. But you and I are perfect together. Come back to me, Casey."

She tried to tug her hand away, but he wouldn't let go, and it felt as if all of Parkvale was pulling on her in a tug-of-war. "Joe, it's over between us. It's too late."

He came around the table and hunkered down in front of her, grasping her knees. "How can it be too late?" he demanded. "A couple of weeks ago you were all set to marry me—so you can't tell me your marriage to this Carmichael guy is the real deal. In your heart, where it matters, nothing's changed at all." He gave her knees a shake to emphasize his point.

Mindful of the curious onlookers at nearby tables, Casey lowered her voice. "Joe, what you did in that TV studio was the exact opposite of chickening out. Until then, you and I were both prepared to settle for something comfortable, a marriage we knew we could live with, rather than risk not finding someone we truly love. You were the one who was brave enough to say that wasn't right."

"It's not like that." Confusion clouded Joe's face. "I do love you, Casey, and I need you. You're the only woman for me. Wherever you want to go, whatever I have to do to make this work, I'll do it."

Coming on the heels of her realization that Adam didn't need her, Joe's words soothed her spirit like a comforting, even tempting, balm. Casey didn't doubt Joe loved her. She shut her eyes, imagined Adam was here. He'd be mouthing, *Tough love,* holding her hand tight, pulling her away.

But Adam wasn't here. She had to do this on her own.

She opened her eyes.

"I'm not coming back, Joe. What you and I had isn't enough for me, and it shouldn't be enough for you."

It took another few minutes to convince him, but at last he left Casey alone with the remains of her lunch. Exhausted, she gulped down her water, patted some of the cool droplets from the rim of the glass on her temples.

She'd actively severed her ties to her family and to Joe.

She was the temporary houseguest of a man who didn't need her.

She felt as if she'd cast herself adrift.

CASEY COULDN'T SETTLE back into her work that afternoon, so she headed out into the garden and busied herself dead-heading the flowering shrubs that grew against the wall between Adam's house and his neighbor's. The work was calming and satisfying, though what Adam's gardener would make of it on his next monthly visit she couldn't be sure.

"Hello there." A voice from above startled her out of her absorption in a camellia bush.

An elderly gentleman peered over the wall, his wrinkled face and blue eyes visible beneath the peak of his orange baseball cap. He had to be standing on a ladder—the wall was about seven feet high. "I'm Bob Harvey," he said.

Casey straightened and pushed her hair back off her perspiring forehead. "Casey Gr-Carmichael," she replied.

"You must be one of the newlyweds. I saw you on TV."

She nodded.

"I don't think I've met your husband."

"He's very busy with work."

He nodded. "Thought that might be it. What about you, do you work?"

Casey ended up spending a pleasant half hour in conversation with Bob. She was still in the garden when Adam came home, late, around eight.

The first clue she had of his arrival was the appearance of his polished black shoes in front of her as she weeded around the base of the sundial.

"You know you don't have to work in the yard." He sounded annoyed.

She looked up. With the sun low in the sky behind him, his face was in shadow. "I'm doing this for relaxation. Sue left a crab salad for dinner if you're hungry."

"Maybe later." His tone more friendly, he said, "If you're ready to stop relaxing, how about a drink?"

She smiled. "Sure, I'll just finish up here."

By the time she'd stowed her tools in the shed and washed her hands, Adam had surprised her by setting up drinks on the back porch. He stood waiting for her, two glasses of chilled white wine on the wrought-iron table. He looked tired, his eyes shadowed, lines visible at the corners of his mouth. He'd been putting in long hours with Sam, working on their legal case, as well as running Carmichael Broadcasting.

Casey sat on the swing seat and patted the space next to her. "If we sit here we'll see the sunset."

He smiled faintly as he settled beside her. "I wouldn't want to miss that."

Casey leaned back and took a sip of her wine. With her foot, she pushed off the ground and set the swing gently rocking. "I met one of your neighbors today. Bob Harvey."

Adam put one foot down. The swing stopped. "I thought I said no neighbors."

"He stuck his head over the wall while I was gardening. I couldn't ignore him."

Adam looked skeptical. "And when are he and Mrs. Harvey coming for dinner?"

She chuckled. "I wouldn't do that to you."

"Good," he said with feeling.

Casey set the swing in motion again. Then Adam said, "How was your lunch with Brodie-Ann?"

"Interesting." She took a long swallow of wine. "She brought Joe along."

Adam stiffened. "The Joe who dumped you on TV?"

"Ouch," she said in mild protest. "Yes, that Joe."

Adam stopped the swing once more and put his glass on the table. He'd figured this would happen, just not so soon. A guy wouldn't let Casey go and not regret it. "I suppose he asked you to go back to him." Adam kept his voice controlled, though he wanted to shout. Dammit, he never shouted.

"How did you know?" Casey ran a finger down the condensation on the outside of her wineglass. She wouldn't meet his eyes; she must have decided to go back to Joe.

"It's obvious," he said contemptuously. "It was only a matter of time before Joe finally realized life was a lot harder without you to look after him."

"You think he can't love me for who I am?" She'd taken his words as an insult, but Adam was too riled to pander to her hurt feelings.

"You mean, he loves you so much he was happy to humiliate you in front of millions of people?"

Casey put her glass down. She made a face, as if her wine suddenly tasted sour. "Don't be horrible."

.Since that abortive lunch at the Peabody, Adam had worked late at the office to stay out of Casey's way. He'd felt closer to her that Sunday than he was comfortable with, and it made sense to put some space between them. But even knowing she was at home and that he would see her in the evening made a difference to his days. That he would lose that before he was ready to, and that Joe would have her back, sent a surge of fury through him.

"I'll bet he knew just the right words to have you running back into his arms," Adam sneered. "Did he tell you he *adores* you?"

"More or less," Casey admitted. "He was very sweet."

"I don't believe this." The swing rocked violently as he stood up. "I shouldn't have let you see Brodie-Ann on your own. I knew something like this would—"

Casey was on her feet now, too. "You don't get to *let* me or not let me do anything, you jerk. I'll decide who I see, I'll decide who my friends are, and I'll decide if I should go back to Joe or not." She was pale with anger, and it made her lips look redder, softer. Had she kissed Joe when she told him she was going back to him?

"You don't make decisions!" Adam roared. So much for never shouting. "You're a pushover, remember? You let people manipulate you with their neediness and their sweet-talking and their adoring. Just don't blame me when you're back in that rut you used to call a life."

Her cheeks flamed with anger, and she clenched her fists at her sides. "I told Joe it was over!" she shouted back. "I told him I wanted more than he could offer. I told him no."

She took the wind out of Adam's sails. He gripped the railing, breathing hard. "Why the hell didn't you say so?"

"You didn't ask, you just assumed." She flounced past him, and he reached out and grabbed her by the elbow.

"What else would I think when you're such a pushover? You'd still be in Parkvale with your sister if I hadn't dragged you out of there the other week."

"I learned something that day," she said. "You showed me how to say no, and today I did it for myself."

He grinned at the pride in her voice—and deliberately shut out the relief that made him almost light-headed. "That's my girl."

"I did it for me, not for you," she said, annoyed.

"Of course." His grin widened. "Sorry I yelled."

She smiled back. "One good thing about you, there's no chance of you manipulating me with sweet talk and neediness and adoring." She sat back down on the swing, and Adam did the same.

"Do you realize we just had our first fight?" Casey turned to look at him and found him closer than she'd thought, his face just inches from hers.

"Do you realize," he parroted, "that your new friend next door probably heard every word of it?"

Casey clapped a hand over her mouth.

"You see," Adam said in a superior tone, "if you'd never met him, it wouldn't bother you. Now you've opened a can of worms, and it's your problem, *darling*."

"Likening Bob Harvey to a can of worms is very rude."

Adam slung an arm over her shoulders. It was casual but nice. "So how do you feel about Joe? It can't have been easy."

She leaned into him, just the tiniest bit. "It was pretty awful. But now I feel…free."

"You're a married woman," he teased. His hand tightened on her shoulder, and a tingling warmth spread down her arm. She looked away from him.

"Joe's the only guy I've ever dated," she said, partly to explain to herself why she reacted so strongly to the unfamiliar excitement of Adam's touch. "I need to learn how to build healthy relationships without getting sucked into that need thing. I guess I should start dating. After our annulment, of course." She patted his knee in reassurance, and left her hand there a moment longer than she should just because it felt good.

Adam's heart stopped. He'd only just gotten over the shock of believing she was going back to Joe, and now she was talking about dating other men.

His reaction to that news, on top of his over-reaction to her lunch with Joe, confirmed that his attraction to Casey was more than physical. He didn't want her thinking about dating other men while she was still living with him. Which meant he had to decide what he did want.

Keep her close…but not too close.

He twirled a strand of her hair around his finger. "You don't have to wait for the annulment."

Her eyes widened. "Our fake marriage won't be very convincing if I start dating other guys."

"You could date me."

Casey's stomach flipped. "Date…you?"

"I was Memphis's most eligible bachelor," he pointed out. "I'm considered quite a catch."

She looked at him, at his tall, graceful physique, the strong planes of his face, his intense blue eyes. "I don't doubt it. So how come you don't have a girlfriend?"

He shrugged. "I haven't met anyone suitable in a while."

There was that word again. "Suitable?"

"Someone who wants to make the most of it when we're together, but doesn't demand a lot in between times. And who's happy to say goodbye when it's over."

It sounded as if he dated the way he did everything else. Logically, with decisive intent.

He smiled, a flash of white teeth. "Like you said, I'm not about to manipulate you or need you."

"When we were staying at the Peabody, you warned me there was no chance of a relationship between us."

"I said a *permanent* relationship," he corrected. "We still have a time limit."

"I want to learn how to date," she said. "What do you want?"

He ran a finger along her jaw. "Do you need to ask? You're a beautiful, sexy—" his voice turned husky "—desirable woman."

Adam wanted her.

"What exactly would dating you involve?"

Her practical question made him smile. "We go out together," he said. "Out for meals. Sometimes, we stay in together. It's not much different from what we do already, except there'll be more of this." He moved closer, so his lips were an inch from hers. "It won't hurt a bit," he promised.

This kiss was more tender than the others. He started at one corner of her mouth, worked his way to the center, then his tongue teased her lips until she parted them. At his slow, stroking entry she found her whole body clenching, and it didn't relax until he hauled her against him and deepened the kiss.

By the time he released her, Casey was shaking. He didn't look a hundred percent steady himself. He raked a hand through his hair, gave her a smile that was part triumphant, part perplexed.

But his voice was calm when he said, "There's one other great thing about dating me."

She raised an eyebrow and, despite the roiling of her insides, said equally calmly, "Only one?"

"If we're trying to convince people we're happily married, this might just do it."

Casey stared straight ahead. As she watched, the sun slipped below the horizon, leaving a glowing pink swath across the sky.

"So, are we dating?" he asked impatiently. "I like you, you like me. And I don't believe you would have kissed just anyone like that."

"Well, maybe not a guy with bad breath and warts on his nose."

"I'm flattered," Adam said dryly. "I had no idea you were so picky."

"I guess," she said, striving for a casual tone though her stomach tied in knots, "we're dating."

CHAPTER NINE

ADAM LOOKED ACROSS his desk at the cluster of people filling his office at ten o'clock on a Wednesday morning. They'd arranged themselves in battle lines—Anna May and Henry to his right, Sam and Eloise to the left.

A faint curl of steam rose from a dish on Adam's desk. Eloise had brought him some of what she called her famous, fresh-baked cornbread. Famous for its ability to drown any man stupid enough to swim after eating it. The stuff weighed a ton. But it was Eloise's mama's secret recipe, and although she had a cook to prepare her meals, Eloise insisted cornbread was her domain. Years ago, Adam had set himself a personal challenge of never eating a bite of the stuff.

He didn't plan to deviate from that this morning, despite being warmly disposed to the world in general, thanks to his newly elevated status as Casey's date.

Anna May glared at Sam as they waited for Adam to speak. She'd said no lawyers for the meeting, a stipulation that suited Adam. But as always, the minute his stepmother entered the building, Sam found a reason to visit Adam's office.

"Well?" Anna May snapped, losing patience.

"Let me get this straight," Adam said. "You're saying that if I promote Henry to joint CEO, give him a bonus equivalent to his first year's salary and agree to pay out a regular dividend to stockholders, backdated for the past three years, you'll drop your legal action to prove Dad was mentally incompetent when he made that will."

From the encouraging nods Sam was sending his way, Adam gathered he was supposed to see Anna May's offer as a good sign. An indication that she feared she might lose and was therefore willing to negotiate. But how good could it be, when his aunt's demands would undermine the financial stability of the business?

Anna May made a dipping, birdlike movement of her head. Vulture-like, Adam thought. He quashed the uncharitable impulse. Somewhere in his aunt's psyche lay the key to her attitude, but he was damned if he knew what it was. It was the sort of thing Casey liked to ponder. The sort of thing Adam didn't have time for.

Maybe he should try doing it Casey's way.

"What made you decide on those particular terms?" he asked Henry.

"We don't want to be unreasonable, Adam," his

cousin said apologetically, "but Mom feels—*we feel*—"

"It's the least Henry's entitled to, according to your father's original will," Anna May interrupted.

Adam and Sam hadn't known about the earlier will before this morning—Adam's father hadn't used Sam for his personal legal work. Anna May had made the most of that, flourishing a copy of the document under their noses. But there was no denying its contents: it divided James Carmichael's stock holdings in Carmichael Broadcasting equally between Adam and Henry.

"But is it what you want?" Adam asked Henry. He'd never seen any sign that his cousin had the same kind of passion for the business that he did. He rephrased the question in Casey-speak. "What are your dreams?"

Henry swallowed nervously. "Actually, I always thought I'd like to—"

"I don't know what this new tactic of yours is, Adam, but it won't work," Anna May said. "We'll be asking the court to overturn your father's will on the grounds that he was mentally unstable when he signed it."

So much for the friendly approach. Adam slipped back into his more familiar, driven mode. "The court will find my father was in his right mind when he wrote his last will," he said, aware of the absurdity of defending a document that he himself planned to challenge, on the basis that his dad couldn't legally insist Adam get married in order to inherit.

He saw Eloise watching him, biting her lip, blinking. He wished she wasn't here, so he could tell Anna May to do her worst. But he figured his aunt had invited Eloise for that very reason. Emotional blackmail. His family was so good at it. Even Dad... When Anna May revealed the contents of the earlier will, Eloise had suggested James had changed it because he'd realized how important his son was to him. Adam would have liked to believe it. But more likely, Dad had seen how much effort Adam was putting into the company, and he'd wanted to be sure that continued.

Adam wished, as he often did, that his dad hadn't asked him to take care of Eloise. It meant he couldn't ignore that his stepmother would be heartbroken to hear her beloved husband labeled crazy in public. But Adam was damned if he was going to cave in a moment before he had to. He turned to his stepmother. "What do you think, Eloise?"

She swallowed, looked over at Anna May, then back at him. "I never give in to blackmail, Adam dear, and nor should you."

What? Adam stared at her, and she inclined her head. He didn't give her a chance to change her mind. "You heard Eloise."

Not the least bit flustered, Anna May got to her

feet, and Henry did the same. "We'll see you in court," she said over her shoulder as she stalked out.

Eloise left a minute later. Sam watched her go with a kind of hopeless despair. "Such a brave woman," he murmured.

For once, Adam had no argument. He pushed the dish of cornbread toward Sam. "Why don't you take this?"

"She made it for you." But the lawyer looked at it hungrily.

"Take it," Adam insisted, and Sam didn't need any further encouragement to drag the dish to his side of the desk.

"How do you rate Anna May's chances with the insanity thing?" Adam asked.

"Less than fifty percent."

Not as low as Adam would have liked. "Surely she can't win on the basis of a couple of stupid remarks I made?"

"I'm betting she'll make a big deal out of your father's failure to notice his accountant stealing money from under his nose," Sam said. "She'll try to link that to a loss of mental competence."

Which would be even more upsetting for Eloise. Adam rubbed his temples.

"This marriage of yours..." Sam said thoughtfully.

"What about it?"

"Is it going well?"

"You tell me. You're the one working on the annulment."

Sam waved that away. "I'm asking if you and Casey get along. It seems to me that you do."

Adam shifted in his seat. If burning up every time he touched his wife, if craving the feel of her lips under his and being aware of every movement of her legs, her hips, counted as getting along, then Sam was right. Adam suspected dating her definitely counted as getting along.

"I'm thinking," Sam said, "that once we beat this insanity thing, the simplest way to deal with Anna May and Henry might be to remove the grounds for their complaint, and drop your challenge to the will."

"How do I do that?" Adam asked.

"You make this marriage for real."

He dropped his pen. "You can't be serious."

Sam nodded, every bit as somber as he always was. "I'm saying this as your friend, not as your lawyer. In the strictly legal sense, I think we'll probably win the battle to have that clause struck out of your father's will. But if you want to do this the easy way…the fact is, you *are* married, and as the will stands you need to be married to inherit. There's a certain synergy."

"There's a certain craziness," Adam retorted. He winced. He'd sworn never to use the words *crazy* or *insane* lightly again.

"Think about it," Sam advised. "If there's any way you and Casey can make a go of it…"

"Not a chance." Adam had to quash the thought before it could take root. So what if he and Casey were dating? He'd dated dozens of women without ever wanting to marry them. He and Casey were poles apart on the things that mattered, with the exception of their mutual exasperation with demanding families. Even if he was interested in making this marriage real—which he wasn't—there was one major obstacle. Casey wanted a man who adored her.

He realized Sam was still talking. "Sorry, what was that?"

"I asked how Eloise is after that fiasco at the Peabody on Sunday. She seemed jumpy this morning."

"I think she's forgiven me," Adam said. He'd phoned his stepmother that night, as Casey suggested. Eloise had still sounded hurt, but also grateful for Adam's call. By the time he hung up, she'd managed a couple of attempts at the lighthearted interference that usually bugged him. This time, he was surprised how relieved he was to know she'd forgiven his indiscretion.

"She's a fine woman." It was a variation on a theme Sam played often.

Adam made a noncommittal sound and added, "She's very loyal to my father's memory."

He didn't intend to warn Sam off. But the attorney had to stop pining for Eloise. He was getting nowhere.

Sam was either in too deep to get the message, or he ignored it. "Time I got going." He stood. "Think about what I said, Adam. Think about how you might convince Casey to stick around."

THE PHONE RANG at eleven o'clock, interrupting Casey just as she neared the end of a chapter.

"Come and join me for lunch." There was no question as to whether she had the time or the inclination. Just a command, delivered in Adam's deep, sexy voice.

"Today?"

"We're dating," he reminded her. "This is what people who date do."

It wasn't something she'd ever done with Joe. Spontaneous lunch dates had never featured in their relationship.

"Be here at twelve."

"Did I ever tell you I prefer new-age guys?" she said. "The kind of guys who ask a woman what she'd like to do?"

"You might suggest something I don't want to do, and then I'd have to refuse," he said. "Just be here at twelve."

Adam hung up before she could argue. If she said too much more, he'd have second thoughts himself.

When he'd suggested last night that they date, he'd planned to take her out for dinner Saturday. The housekeeper had the day off, and they had to eat. He'd had no plans of lunching with Casey until Sam had said his piece about keeping this marriage going. Then a crazy impulse had made him pick up the phone.

Doesn't matter, he told himself. Whether he was just dating her for fun or they were going to make this marriage real, it made sense to start right away.

THEY SAT CLOSE to the riverbank in a secluded area of Ashburn Coppack Park that afforded a spectacular view of the downtown skyline.

"I can't believe you thought of this," Casey said. She grinned, then noticed his hesitation before he smiled back.

"I may be practical, but I'm not totally lacking imagination," he said.

She crossed one leg over the other. The movement drew Adam's gaze, as she knew it would, to the shortness of the light green linen skirt she'd chosen for just that reason, and which she'd teamed with an off-the-shoulder white cotton top. She'd spent half an hour trying on and discarding different outfits, and wanted to be sure he appreciated her final choice. "This is the perfect place for a picnic."

"Perfect," he agreed, his gaze still on her legs.

Casey couldn't quite believe how wholeheartedly Adam had thrown himself into this dating thing. Barely twelve hours after she'd consented to the idea, he'd conjured up a picnic—at least, his secretary had—and driven them to the park, insisting Casey should leave her car at his office.

Adam threw a piece of bread to a passing duck, then helped himself to more potato salad out of one of the deli containers. He could get used to this.

The food was delicious, the chilled bottle of white wine relaxing, and as for the company...

If there was one thing he would take from this month with Casey, Adam reflected, it was renewed pleasure in the simple things in life. Like picnics, sunsets and conversation. Over lunch, he and Casey had talked about everything and nothing, from the new family drama series about to debut on Channel Eight, to a plotting problem she was having in her book. They'd even digressed to a game that involved naming as many towns as they could think of on the Mississippi. He won. At least, he thought he had.

He looked at the potato salad on his plate and realized he wasn't the least bit hungry. He'd already had dessert, a slice of key lime pie. Going back for a second helping of potato salad was, as Casey would say in her quack psychoanalytic way, substitution.

He slid a sideways glance at her, lying on the blanket, eyes closed, face raised to the sun. Her hands were clasped behind her head, a pose that lifted her breasts against the thin cotton of her blouse and shortened that skirt even farther. Strands of silky hair fell over her arms and grazed the blanket. A smile hovered on her mouth.

As if sensing his scrutiny, Casey moistened her lips with her tongue. Adam swung his gaze back to the potato salad. Yep, right now, he was substituting potato salad for a taste of his wife's lips.

Think about how you might convince Casey to stick around, Sam had said.

The most obvious way to do that, Adam had decided, was to take their relationship to the next level. Sex. And, dammit, he hadn't been able to think about anything else since. Not that the idea hadn't occurred to him before Sam started dispensing his advice so freely. But back then, Adam had been able to slap it away as totally inappropriate. Now, it was as if Sam had given him permission to think about having Casey in his bed, about all the things he'd like to do to her there.

Not that he'd even decided he wanted her to stick around. He should probably discuss Sam's suggestion with her.

Trouble was, talking was the last thing on his mind now. The memory of the sweetness of her mouth was driving him crazy.

"Adam?" Casey propped herself up on her elbows, and the movement lifted her breasts even more. There was a languidness in her voice that he found infinitely seductive. "It's sweltering. Can you please pass the water bottle?"

He did as she asked, then stifled a groan as she tipped her head back and, eyes shut, drank greedily, so that a trickle of water escaped the side of her mouth to run down her chin and throat. He touched a finger there to stem the flow, and found her pulse beating.

Casey's eyes opened and he saw heat in their depths, which the water had done nothing to cool. Without looking away, she put the bottle down beside her. Adam slipped his hand around the back of her neck and pulled her up toward him, so their mouths were an inch apart.

He didn't rush into the kiss. He'd been here before and he knew how right it felt. Now that he had her so close, he wanted to savor every second. Her eyes fluttered shut again as his lips drifted against hers.

But the instant their mouths met he could think of nothing but how much he wanted her, and his intended gentleness evaporated. Casey's lips parted to welcome his tongue. She moaned as he deepened the kiss, and she struggled to pull herself upright so she could press herself closer to him.

The hunger in Adam had its epicenter in one obvious place. He moved a hand to cup a full, rounded breast. He felt the tensing of her body, and his mouth absorbed her sigh.

Her arms wound around his neck, and Adam slipped his other hand beneath her shirt to caress her back. He wanted nothing more than to tear every stitch of clothing off her and make love to her. Now.

Then some small corner of his mind remembered they were in a public place.

Home. If he could somehow convince his mouth to move away from hers, he would tell her to get in the car, so they could go home right away and continue this in private. Her protest when he finally managed to pull away almost destroyed the last shreds of his restraint.

"Let's go home," he croaked.

CHAPTER TEN

WORDLESSLY, THEY THREW the take-out containers, plates and food scraps into the picnic basket. The blanket was bundled in as well, then they were racing for the Aston Martin.

Adam kissed Casey again as they fumbled to do up their seat belts, a searing kiss intended to remind them both why were they were in such a hurry—not that he'd forgotten.

He hit the road for home, driving as fast as he dared.

Casey turned up the fan on her side. "If we go home now, we'll go to bed, right?"

Bed, floor, kitchen table… Adam realized with a shock he didn't mind where they did it. "Yep," he said. Had he ever wanted someone this badly?

"Which would mean we'd be sleeping together on our first date." She squirmed in her seat.

"Nope."

"No?"

"No sleeping," he said. "Definitely no sleeping."

She sucked in a breath. "The thing is," she said, "I don't do that on a first date."

Adam slowed for a red light ahead. He turned to her, saw her anxiously gnawing her lip. "You don't have a first-date routine," he reminded her.

"If I did, this wouldn't be in it," she insisted.

The light turned green and Adam accelerated the car, but without the same urgency.

"Would *you* normally do that on a first date?" she asked.

"We're married," he said. "I see you every day. Hell, I've probably seen more of you than I did the last six women I dated combined."

Casey stared out the window. "Joe is the only man I've slept with."

Yeah, and didn't Adam want to punch the guy.

"You're scared," he said.

"I need some time to get used to the idea."

"How much time?"

"How much time will you give me?"

He waited until he'd passed an old lady whose Toyota was weaving down the center of the road before he answered. "It's not about what I'll give you. It's about when you think you can decide what you want."

"Why don't you come over to my place for dinner tonight?"

Suddenly everything looked brighter again. "Second date," he said. "Great idea."

CASEY STARED UNSEEING at her computer keyboard, unable to connect with the words on the screen in front of her, the chapter she'd aimed to finish today.

The heat of that kiss in the park had seared through her, destroying her focus.

In her seven years with Joe, Casey had never known the overwhelming desire Adam had ignited in her today. She'd spent three weeks with him, and was ready to make love. To Casey that had to mean she was in danger of losing her heart to him.

Which wouldn't be a problem, if he lost his to her in return.

She tried to evaluate the odds of that happening. Adam wasn't a lose-his-heart kind of guy. But she knew she hadn't imagined the deeper connection between them. Maybe if they got closer, if they made love, they could move ahead emotionally.

Casey looked at her watch. Four o'clock. She'd promised to visit Eloise this afternoon. She would make it quick, then come home to prepare for an evening with Adam—when they would pick up where they'd left off at lunchtime. Her stomach fluttered.

AN UNFAMILIAR CAR was parked outside Eloise's front door when Casey arrived.

Eloise welcomed her inside. "Sam Magill is visiting," she said in a low, vexed voice. "He's just gone to the bathroom." She led Casey into a spacious living room, sunlit through a double set of French doors and dominated by a huge fireplace, above which hung an enormous gilded mirror. "He came to see if I need any help dead-heading my roses—though what he thinks I employ a gardener for, I don't know." She shook her head. "That man thinks I'm incapable of looking after myself. It's insulting."

Casey felt a surge of sympathy for the lovelorn lawyer. And a rush of resentment for the emotional independence that Eloise and Adam were so determined, each in their own way, to cling to.

"Most men as good-looking as Sam are too selfish to worry about other people," she told Eloise. "I'll bet he has a whole bunch of women after him."

Casey had noticed Eloise's friends eyeing him at lunch last weekend. Sam was tall, in good shape, with rugged features. And he was single, in an age group where men were in increasingly short supply.

Eloise stopped short. "Is Sam good-looking?" she asked, astounded.

"I'm told I am," Sam said from behind them.

Eloise gave a little scream. "Sam Magill, what are you doing, sneaking up like that? You should know better than…"

She trailed off as she looked at Sam—really looked at him—as if for the first time. She blinked, then blinked again. Color stole up her neck and over her face, and her hand fluttered at her chest.

It was obvious Sam didn't know how to react to the scrutiny of the woman he'd admired so long. He stood there in the middle of the living room, saying nothing, with all the eloquence of a sack of potatoes. Casey longed to give him a nudge, to tell him to jump in and ask Eloise on a date.

"Well." Her mother-in-law regained her senses and spoke briskly. "I daresay you're passably handsome. But that's neither here nor there." She turned toward the door in an unmistakable signal that the lawyer should leave. "I surely do appreciate your dropping in, Sam, but I'm fine and so are my roses."

He looked so downcast, Eloise gave him a reprieve. "Just one moment while I fetch you a jar of my pear preserves. I still do them myself every year."

That she hurried out of the room was interesting in itself, Casey reflected. Eloise considered hurrying unladylike.

Casey decided she didn't have time to pull any punches. "You're going about it the wrong way," she told Sam. "Eloise thinks you're interfering."

"I only want to help," he protested, once he got over his initial shock at her direct approach. "She's on her own and must need the occasional piece of advice. But every time I open my mouth…"

"You mess up because you're trying too hard," Casey said.

He moved over to the mantelpiece, stared down

at the empty grate. "I just want to do something for her. To earn her…respect."

They both knew he wanted a whole lot more than respect. Casey recognized the problem. Sam figured Eloise had to need him before she would fall for him.

"What Eloise *needs* is company, someone to share the ups and downs with," she said. "Then maybe, eventually, someone to love."

Sam looked doubtful.

"It's worth a try," Casey said awkwardly.

He harrumphed in a way that might have meant he would give it some thought, or that he didn't want to talk about it. His eyes met Casey's in the mirror above the fireplace. "While we're on the subject of who likes whom," he said, "you and Adam appear to be getting along."

She nodded.

"If you want to do something for him—" Sam turned to face her "—stay married to him."

Her heart raced. "Why do you say that?"

"If you two stay together, Adam won't need to challenge his father's will."

Casey licked her suddenly dry lips. "I don't think Adam wants to stay married to me." But that didn't stop her pulse from jumping, her breath going shallow. She heard the click of Eloise's heels out in the foyer and exhaled slowly.

Sam had heard Eloise, too, and he added in a rush, "He didn't sound opposed to it."

"You...you suggested this to Adam?"

Sam nodded.

"When was that?" *Please, let it be after lunch today.*

"This morning, right after we met with Anna May."

Eloise arrived with a large jar of pears, which Sam accepted with effusive thanks. He clutched it to his chest as if it were the key to Fort Knox. Eloise escorted him to the front door, giving Casey precious seconds to pull herself together.

Giving her time to face the cold, hard truth.

When Adam had started his seduction today, it had been with Sam's suggestion in mind.

She closed her eyes, sick to her stomach. Whatever that kiss had been about, it hadn't been as simple as him wanting her.

It never was.

ADAM LEFT THE OFFICE at five o'clock for the first time in years. Combined with his extended lunch hour, that made it the shortest working day he could remember.

Not short enough.

All afternoon he'd been able to think of nothing except Casey. He'd never been so preoccupied by a woman that his chief accountant had had to ask him a question three times.

It was worryingly reminiscent of his father and Eloise. But Adam figured he'd take the edge off his distraction as soon as he went to bed with Casey.

She wasn't home when he got there, and the place felt empty. He called Eloise, who told him Casey had just left. That meant another ten minutes. He busied himself setting the table for dinner, pouring wine, serving the meal the housekeeper had left.

When Casey finally arrived, he wanted to haul her into his arms and get started right then.

But this was supposed to be a date, and she'd made it clear she didn't want to be rushed. So instead, he kissed her briefly and said, "Dinner's ready."

At first, when she didn't say much through the meal, he figured it was because she was as distracted as he was. But gradually he noticed little details—the dip at the corners of her mouth, the shadow in her eyes.

Adam got a sinking feeling.

He didn't want to get into one of those emotional discussions. For what felt like the umpteenth time recently, he did something he didn't want to do. He ignored the warning bell in his head. "Is something wrong?" he asked.

She dropped her gaze, apparently intensely interested in her baked fish and scalloped potatoes. "I've been thinking about what we said this afternoon, and I don't think we should...you know."

"If you're worried this will affect our annulment, Sam found out the nonconsummation thing is mainly used in church annulments. Our case is based on the fact we didn't know it was a real marriage."

"Adam," she said, "Sam told me he talked to you about us staying married for real."

He put down his knife and fork. "I was going to talk to you about that."

"Before we made love, or after?"

"After I'd figured out whether I thought it was a good idea," he said. "It had nothing to do with you and me going to bed."

When she glared at him, he said, "Okay, maybe it did...speed things up a bit. But you know I wanted you before that. I wanted you the day I met you, though maybe I didn't acknowledge it then. I want you now."

Casey didn't know what to believe. What had he said to her the day they'd met? That people should know what they want and go after it. *He could at least pretend he cares.* She pulled herself up short. She'd said she didn't want to be loved just for what she could do for a man—the implied corollary being that she wanted to be loved for herself. But wasn't it equally true that if Adam wanted to ask something of her, he should do it honestly, without pretending it involved love?

"What did you decide...about Sam's suggestion?"

Adam shifted in his chair. "It has its pros and cons."

"Would you like to share those with me?"

"No," he said. "I'd like to go to bed with you."

He hadn't said *make love*.

"Very much," he added. When she didn't respond, he said, "More than I've ever wanted to before." He sounded surprised, yet about as excited as if he was discussing the scheduling of this week's TV movies. Maybe even less excited. Then he added, "I know you want the same thing."

"On…" Casey's voice came out raspy, so she cleared her throat and tried again, striving for the same detachment. "On one level, that's true." She saw the flare of triumph in his eyes. "But wanting it doesn't mean it's a good idea."

He pushed his chair back and stood, then walked around to her side of the table, his tread deliberate, intent. Casey was forced to lean back in her seat to meet his gaze. He loomed over her, searching her face with smoldering eyes, and the masculine heat that emanated from him scorched Casey's nerve endings. He hadn't touched her yet.

He rectified that by pulling her from her seat. Leaning against the edge of the table, he stationed her between his legs, facing him, his hard thighs around hers to keep her in place. His hands clasped her waist, not tightly, but with enough possessiveness to tell her he wouldn't readily let her go.

"I don't know if it's a good idea for us to stay married," he said, "but I do know this is a good idea."

He dipped his head, took her mouth with certitude. Beguiled by his tongue's provocative exploration, Casey lost the thread of her argument. She opened to his moist caress, felt a thick warmth spread through her, deadening any senses that weren't employed in touching and tasting Adam.

He flicked the buttons of her shirt undone, parted it to reveal her breasts, full and aching in her lacy bra. His eyes darkened, and when he lowered his mouth there, she thought her legs might collapse from under her. She leaned into him, felt his unmistakable hardness, and clutched at his hair.

"Sweetheart," he breathed, as his hands moved to the zipper of her skirt.

For the briefest instant, she reveled in the endearment. Then the voice of reason whispered, *He doesn't mean it.*

Casey wanted to scream, to drown out the thought. But she couldn't ignore it. She tugged on Adam's hair, lifting his head so she could see his eyes. "Stop," she said.

To her surprise, the word came out with sufficient authority that Adam did stop. He straightened, put some space between them as Casey did up the buttons of her blouse, trying to ignore the scrape of her fingers against the oversensitized skin of her breasts.

"I'm not going to make love to you," she said. "It'll complicate everything and I won't be able to decide what I want. You know that, and you're using sex to manipulate me."

His eyes darkened again, this time with anger. "I'm not like your family or your boyfriend. I want you, you want me—it can be that simple, if you'll let it."

She folded her arms. "I'm not a pushover anymore."

For a long moment, he stared at her. Then he grasped her by the shoulders, planted a swift, hard kiss on her mouth. "I'll wait."

CHAPTER ELEVEN

"YOU KNOW, MY DEAR, I had quite given up on Adam marrying until you came along." Eloise stirred sugar into her coffee, then tossed the spoon with practiced ease across the kitchen to land in the sink.

When she'd first tried that maneuver a couple of weeks earlier, the spoon had hit the window behind the sink and cracked it. Since then, she'd taken to calling in on Casey most days, and now, by the start of the fourth week of their friendship, her aim had improved remarkably.

Casey smiled, managing not to cringe at the reference to marriage, and continued preparing the seafood salad. It was the housekeeper's day off. Adam had suggested they dine out, but Casey had declined. He hadn't called it a date, but she suspected it was part of his campaign to get her into bed. As far as she was concerned, all dates were off. As extra insurance against temptation, she'd invited Eloise for dinner on several occasions, tonight included.

"Now, Eloise," she chided the older woman. "You hadn't given up at all. I know all about your bridefest."

Eloise chortled. "Adam used that awful word just to annoy me."

"Are you saying you weren't trying to find him a wife?"

Eloise almost succeeded in looking insulted. "Not at all." At Casey's snort she added, "All right, I introduced him to various young women I thought I could tolerate as a daughter-in-law. I just wanted him to know the happiness I once did. But I knew it would take a miracle." Her eyes misted. "And then you came along."

Uncomfortable, Casey turned the conversation back to Eloise. "Were you very much in love with Adam's father?"

The older woman's face lit up. "Oh, yes. I miss James every day, but I thank God for the time we had. We'd only been married six years when he had that heart attack, and then a stroke right after." She shuddered. "We were in bed—just reading, my dear," she assured Casey, who really didn't want to know.

"Next minute, I was dialing 911, and the ambulance crew was saying I was lucky I hadn't lost him already."

"So he died that night?" Casey asked.

Eloise shook her head. "He recovered, quite

well. The stroke slowed his speech, and he couldn't move his right side much, but they ran all kinds of scans and tests, which showed no damage to anything that mattered. I thought I'd be taking him home with me in a few days' time."

"Then what?" Casey asked, though the weight of grief in Eloise's voice gave her the answer.

"A week later, he had another heart attack." Eloise dabbed a handkerchief to her eyes. "We only had those few years together, but, my, they were wonderful. Every one of them was worth a decade with an ordinary man."

"Do you think you'll ever marry again?" Casey asked. If Sam could only stop making a fool of himself every time he got near Eloise, he might be a good match for her, with his old-world manners and his obvious desire to cherish her.

Eloise shook her head. "I was forty-two when I married James, a spinster and perfectly happy that way. I don't believe the man exists who could measure up to him, and I'm not prepared to settle for less."

"Good for you." Casey meant it. She could learn something from Eloise about not settling. Still, she decided to have one last try at advancing Sam's cause. "Eloise, I know you have lots of friends and you're busy. But sometimes I catch something in your face…. You look lonely."

Eloise read Casey's concern, and it warmed her. Her daughter-in-law was such a sweet thing—Eloise hoped Adam knew how lucky he was. She suspected he didn't. Not yet. Whatever the truth behind Casey's and Adam's marriage, it wasn't what the world saw. But a boy as smart as Adam would eventually realize he'd chosen the right bride, and would do what he needed to make the marriage work.

"I won't say I don't get lonely," she told Casey. "Of course I do. But what I had with James… I can't replace that."

"Was he the possessive type?"

Eloise shook her head. "He didn't need to be. I never had eyes for anyone else."

"I wondered," Casey said, "if you thought maybe he wouldn't want you to find someone else."

"My dear, it's not him, it's me," Eloise said, hastening to quash any implication that James might have been less than the generous, loving man he was. "I'm just…better on my own."

Though if that was so, why on earth had that stuffy Sam been occupying her thoughts to such an alarming extent, ever since she'd taken a look at him last week and realized Casey was right? The man was handsome. Very handsome. She should have noticed that before. Then it wouldn't be bothering her the way it did now.

Eloise fanned her face against a sudden heat that had nothing to do with the late afternoon sun streaming into the kitchen. She was behaving like a silly girl whose head had been turned by a dash of male attention. So what if Sam liked her, in a way that was annoyingly, yet quite endearingly, inept? He wasn't James.

James isn't here.

Eloise tamped down the traitorous thought. She loved James and always would.

"The thing about Sam," she said to Casey, "is he acts as if I do everything wrong. If I ever wanted another man, which I don't, I'd want someone who wants to love me, not to improve me or organize me. Someone who wants what I have to offer. Which is love. Only love." She smiled at her daughter-in-law. "Really, what could be better than that?"

Casey didn't know how to answer. In her experience, few people wanted only love. They wanted love plus housekeeping. Love plus babysitting.

Never just love.

Sometimes not even love.

Eloise's face softened. "I do wish we'd had longer, so James and Adam could have reconciled. Adam blamed James for his mother's death, you know."

Casey tipped the tomato she'd just chopped into the salad bowl. "He says his father changed when he met you."

Eloise nodded. "After I met him, James was ashamed of the way he'd behaved toward his family. His own parents were cold and distant, and he married Adam's mother for the worst of reasons—her family's money—and made no secret of it. By his own admission, he was a lousy husband, and a poor father to Adam."

"It must have been hard for Adam, to see his father so loving toward you."

"So you've noticed I'm not Adam's favorite person?" Eloise laughed at Casey's stricken expression. "My dear, you can understand where he's coming from. I didn't find out about the financial mess James was in until he died, so Adam must have thought me utterly profligate. He was probably right. He wouldn't touch a penny of his father's life insurance to rebuild the business. He said I'd need that for myself. There I was, living the life I'd always lived, while that boy worked like a dog to rescue Carmichael Broadcasting from a disaster he blames me for."

"It wasn't your fault." Casey whisked balsamic vinegar in a jug, together with some olive oil.

"Adam felt betrayed," Eloise said gently. She slid the salt and pepper across the island to Casey. "James taught him that the business came first, that family was a distant second. Then, just as Adam finally had the chance to get close to his father at work, James changed the rules on him.

"Then he made that foolish will, which meant Adam ended up more annoyed than grieved when his dad died. I tried to convince James to change the will after his stroke, but he refused.

"But then you came along," Eloise said briskly. She drank the last of her coffee. "And dear Adam will have the happiness he deserves."

"Adam and I... It's early days. We're still getting to know each other." Maybe Casey could prepare Eloise for the blow she would suffer when the annulment came through.

"Of course you are, my dear. It must be so exciting. But one only has to look at the two of you together to see how right you are." Tears glistened in her eyes, and she blew her nose delicately. "I'll just wash my hands, dear."

When Casey heard the kitchen door open a minute later, she assumed Eloise had returned. Without turning around, she said, "How do you know when two people are right together?"

"When wanting the other person keeps you awake at night," Adam said.

Casey squawked and spun around. "When did you come in?"

"Just now." He walked up to her, so close he could kiss her, but he didn't. "How long have you been talking to yourself? You know that's a sign you're not getting enough sleep."

"Wanting you does not keep me awake at night," she said, as crushingly as she could.

"You mean you've been stockpiling sleep?" he asked. "In that case, why not spend tonight with me? We can stay awake all night long."

He put his hands on her waist, closed the gap between them. His eyes blazed down at her.

"I won't be in your bed," she said. "Other than in your dreams."

"Hmm, let me show you how my dreams start." He kissed her, long and hard, until she opened her mouth to him. He walked her to the counter, deepening the kiss so that her head dropped back, revealing her throat. With a murmur of appreciation he left her mouth and started kissing her neck.

"Ahem," Eloise said from the doorway.

Adam cursed and sprang away from Casey. "What's she doing here?" He obviously realized that sounded rude even for him, and said, "Sorry, Eloise, you startled me."

"Evidently," she told him serenely. "Casey invited me to stay for dinner. But if you two would rather be alone…"

"No," Casey said quickly. "We want you to stay. I thought after dinner we could…play Monopoly."

"If that's what you'd like, dear," Eloise said. "Though Monopoly does take rather a long time."

"Does it?" Casey asked.

"Enthralling though that sounds," Adam said, "I need to go back to the office after dinner."

"I'll stay and keep you company then," Eloise offered happily. She reached for Casey's hand, squeezed it. "Truly, dear, getting to know you has been a wonderful treat. It seems odd to say this when I've known you such a short time, but already I love you like a daughter."

Casey returned Eloise's impulsive hug, because she couldn't look her in the eye.

Eloise was offering the no-strings love Casey had always wanted. A gift she couldn't accept, because she was an impostor.

Behind Eloise, Casey saw Adam's startled recognition of what his stepmother was offering...and something that looked very much like envy.

ADAM COULDN'T EXPLAIN his somber mood next morning. All he knew was that touching scene between Casey and Eloise had left him feeling as if he was missing out on something. He didn't want to think about what that was.

"Is anything wrong?" he asked Casey, in an attempt to get out of his own head. She looked about as cheerful as he felt.

She put down her cup of tea. "Adam, I don't know how to tell you this."

For one awful moment he feared something might have happened to Eloise. "What is it?"

"Sue—the housekeeper. She called last night after you went back to work. She quit."

Relief washed over him. He looked at Casey, rubbed his chin.

"Say something," she demanded.

"You must be doing something right."

"Right? How do you mean?"

"As I recall, Mrs. Lowe lasted approximately forty-eight hours after you moved in. Sue lasted, what—two weeks? That's a huge improvement."

Casey smiled reluctantly. "It's not funny, Adam. I have no idea why she left. I'm starting to think it's me."

"No way, darling," he teased her. "I distinctly recall you telling me you've never upset anyone in your life. Right before Mrs. Lowe left, I think it was."

She huffed in protest, and suddenly he was smiling again. It felt good to have a problem as trivial as who would take care of the house.

THURSDAY HAD A RED CIRCLE around it on the calendar in Adam's kitchen. It was the first round of the court battle with Anna May and Henry. Today, Anna May hoped to convince a judge that enough evidence of James Carmichael's mental incompetence existed that the case deserved a full hearing.

Casey cooked eggs and bacon for Adam's breakfast, wishing there was something she could do to ensure that Anna May's farcical motion never got beyond today's preliminary hearing. Eloise was dreading the media coverage, and Adam didn't need this on top of everything else.

He ate his breakfast in silence, then gathered up his briefcase and cell phone. "I'll call and let you know how it goes."

Casey stood. "Good luck." And before she could question the wisdom of it—before Adam could back away—she grabbed hold of his lapels and leaned in to kiss him.

It was meant to be a brief peck. But she ought to know by now that a quick taste of Adam's mouth was never enough. She moved closer, all but plastered herself to the length of him, and parted her lips.

Adam got the hint. His tongue claimed hers and he dragged her close, and Casey relished the weight of him pressing against her.

When he broke away, he kept ahold of her shoulders. "Thanks. I feel a lot better."

The intense heat in his eyes unnerved her. "That was for luck," she joked. "They call me Lucky Lips."

With his thumb, he traced the outline of her mouth, sending an erotic message straight to her core.

"Whoever 'they' are," he said, "I hope they know I'm the only man entitled to these lips."

For now.

He didn't say those words and neither did Casey. But they hung between them like neon lights, illuminating the tenderness of the moment and revealing it to be false.

Casey stepped out of his embrace. "I'll go see Eloise while you're in court." Adam had asked his stepmother not to attend the hearing, and she'd gladly agreed. Casey wouldn't go either, since, as Adam's bride, she was a sore reminder to Anna May that Adam had fulfilled the will's conditions.

As she drove to Eloise's, Casey fretted over how the older woman must feel. She'd been through so much. To finally meet her soul mate, then to have him suffer a heart attack and a stroke just a few years later… And just when Eloise had thought James might recover, he'd—

"That's it!" Casey thumped her car's ancient steering wheel in excitement. Eloise had mentioned all those tests James had undergone after his stroke. *They must have included tests on his brain.*

Casey pulled out her cell phone and called her stepmother-in-law. A car honked behind her—not because the driver thought she was sexy, but because she'd strayed into the next lane. Casey got the Fiesta under control while she waited for Eloise to answer.

Eloise caught on fast to her garbled questioning. She promised to have the information Casey needed by the time she arrived. Next, Casey phoned Adam. But his cell phone was switched off. So was Sam's. She would have to go to the courthouse.

Fifteen minutes later, Eloise had made two calls to the hospital that had treated James, and one to her late husband's lawyer. The news was all good. She insisted on coming with Casey to the courthouse. "I'll park the car, dear, while you run in."

The hearing was scheduled for ten o'clock. Technically, it wouldn't matter if they were late, but Casey wanted to stop it before it even started. She wanted there to be no public mention of James Carmichael being unhinged.

They made it with ten minutes to spare. Eloise gamely took over the controls of the Fiesta, while Casey raced inside. She found Adam with Sam Magill outside courtroom number one. Across the hall, Anna May and Henry waited with all three of their lawyers.

Adam's eyebrows shot up when he saw her. "I thought we said…"

Casey was tempted to shout out that she had evidence Adam's dad wasn't crazy. But it occurred to her that some of the people milling around the hallway were likely journalists who'd enjoy provoking a discussion about the sanity of one of Memphis's benefactors. So she pulled Adam and a bemused Sam into a huddle.

She told them how Eloise had called the psychiatrist who'd tested James after his stroke, and how the man was certain James was fully competent.

"We knew that," Sam said. "What matters is James's state of mind when he wrote his will."

Casey delivered her pièce de résistance. "Eloise told me that after the stroke, she asked James to change his will. He had his lawyer bring it in so he could review it. In the end, he decided he was happy with it as it was. Thanks to the psychiatric tests he'd just had, we know the will reflects the thinking of a sane man."

"We do," Sam agreed, surprised but pleased. "But surely if we knew this…"

"Eloise forgot about James reviewing the will until she mentioned it to me on Monday," Casey said, "and even then she didn't make the link between that and the psych tests."

Adam grabbed Casey by the upper arms. "You," he said, "are incredible." Then he kissed her, right there. Not quite the bone-shaking kiss they'd shared this morning, but with enough heat to cause Henry to clear his throat across the hall.

By the time they surfaced for air, Sam was in close discussions with the other side's legal team and Eloise was strolling through the courthouse doors with a spring in her step more suited to a garden party.

Five minutes later, a triumphant Sam announced that Anna May had conceded Casey's evidence outweighed anything she could present to the judge today. The hearing would be cancelled. Even Anna May's threat that they hadn't heard the last of this couldn't dampen their triumph.

"That's marvelous, Sam," Eloise said, laying a palm on his arm. When she realized what she'd done, her eyes widened. But before she could whip her hand away, Sam covered it with his own.

"How about we adjourn to the café next door for a celebratory coffee?" he said. "Maybe even one with caffeine, Eloise, if your blood pressure is up to it."

She stiffened, and Casey braced herself for the usual retort that would singe Sam's ego. But for once, he appeared to have realized exactly how he sounded, for he darted a look of apology at Eloise. "On second thought, I bow to your superior knowledge in these matters. You choose."

It was obvious Eloise liked that. A smile played at the corners of her mouth.

"Coffee, my foot," she said. "It's gone ten o'clock. This calls for champagne."

To his credit, Sam refrained from expressing any concern about the state of Eloise's liver, or about the wisdom of buying champagne when an American sparkling wine would be better value for money. Instead he bowed, a gesture made awkward by the fact that he wouldn't relinquish his grip on Eloise's hand, and escorted her out the door.

Adam tucked Casey's hand through his own arm as they left the building. "Thanks," he said. "What you did today went way beyond our agreement. I owe you."

CHAPTER TWELVE

WHEN THE PHONE RANG at some unearthly hour on Saturday morning, Casey pulled her pillow over her head to block out the noise.

But Adam's shout pierced her feather-and-cotton shelter. He thumped on the door of her bedroom, and before she could tell him to wait, in he stormed.

He was brandishing the morning newspaper. "Eloise called to say we should take a look at this."

Casey sat up in bed and tried to ignore the fact that his white terry-cloth robe hung open to reveal his bare chest—a frankly yummy chest, its muscled firmness accentuated by just the right amount of dark, curling hair—and black boxers sitting snugly on his hips.

She wasn't doing a very good job of ignoring it—he had to clear his throat to get her attention. The appreciation wasn't all one-sided, Casey realized as she followed the direction of his gaze and looked down at her nightdress. The thin straps had slipped off her shoulders, and the way she was leaning forward didn't leave anything to the imagination.

Casey grimaced and tugged her nightie back into place before she took the paper and read the headline: TV Couple's Wedding a Sham.

"Oh no!" A wedding photo—of her and Adam kissing—had pride of place on the front page. Around it were smaller photos of the two of them, taken, if she wasn't wrong, right here in this house. "How did they—?" The photo at the bottom answered the question. It was their erstwhile house-keeper, Sue Mason. Only the picture was captioned, "Sue O'Connor, undercover journalist."

"How bad is it?" Casey couldn't bear to read the words that laid open their private lives—their private *lies*—to the world.

"About what you'd expect." Adam scanned the article for what he presumably considered a choice extract, and read aloud. "'Adam and Casey Carmichael, a doting couple in the public eye, sleep in separate bedrooms and seldom exchange more than the merest courtesies.'"

"That's not true," Casey protested. "I mean, the bedroom part is, but how dare she say you're courteous?"

"Do you think this is funny?" he said.

She shook her head. "If I don't laugh, I'll cry." Her voice cracked on the last word. She squeezed her eyes shut, picturing her family reading this stuff and knowing the truth.

"It's not all bad," Adam soothed her. "Listen to

this. 'Casey Carmichael is a kind and considerate employer, who always has a smile on her face. But one senses that beneath the vibrant facade—'" He stopped.

"What does it say?"

"Uh, nothing, it's just—"

Casey snatched the newspaper from him and quickly found where he'd left off. "'One senses that beneath the vibrant facade is a woman hurt by her husband's indifference.'" She stared at Adam. "I don't know if that's worse for me or for you."

"For you," he said immediately. "It makes you sound pathetic."

"It makes you sound nasty," she pointed out. "I'd rather be pathetic than nasty."

"But any self-respecting man would rather be nasty than pathetic."

"That explains a lot," she muttered. She pushed her quilt aside and climbed out of bed. On the way to fetch her robe, she detoured to the window to open the shutters.

"Casey, don't." Adam rushed to stop her, but it was too late.

She froze. Adam must have left the gates open last night because the front garden was a seething mass of journalists. When the crowd saw her and Adam at the window, the photographers raised their cameras and began snapping away.

By BREAKFAST TIME Sunday, Adam was starting to feel as if they were on a rerun of their honeymoon. Only this time around, even though they had a whole house to share, being shut in with Casey was even greater torment.

He sighed. Was it too much to hope that something more newsworthy had happened in Memphis overnight to drag the media away from his front yard?

He turned from the toaster to ask, "How are the headlines today?"

Casey read from the front page of the Sunday paper. "'Love or Lies? Carmichaels in hiding.'" She showed him the picture—of her in her nightgown, openmouthed at the bedroom window, with Adam behind her, his expression dark. "This paper claims the other guys got it wrong, judging by the fact that we appeared at the same window together, half-clothed."

"They just wish they'd thought of coming in undercover themselves." Adam took the opportunity to inhale Casey's fresh, morning fragrance as he stepped closer to scan the article. He grimaced at the rampant speculations it contained. "I wish these people had something better to do. We need a real disaster the press can focus on, something else to fill the front pages."

"Earthquake? Political assassination?" Casey suggested helpfully.

"I didn't say I wanted anyone to die. Some fraudster conning old ladies out of their fortunes would do. He could start with Eloise."

"Adam! You don't want that to happen. You know you'd feel obliged to come to her rescue."

"Very funny." Not only would he feel obliged to help Eloise, these days he'd actually want to. Adam turned back to the toaster. "How do you like your toast?"

"Toasted," Casey said.

"What does that mean?"

"It means however it comes. How many ways are there to have toast?"

"There's well done, medium and light," he said. "But pardon me for asking."

He gathered from her humph that she'd never heard such a dumb question. That's what a guy got when he tried to be considerate. Life was so much easier before he'd started…liking Casey.

"We need a strategy," he said.

"Are you still talking about toast?" she asked ominously.

"I'm talking about proving our marriage is genuine."

"You can't prove something that's not true," she objected.

"If you think I'm going to let all of Memphis believe I'm not capable of making my wife happy—"

"Didn't you say it's cool to be nasty?"

"I said it's better than being pathetic. But if they're going to imply it's my fault you and I aren't sleeping together…"

She laughed out loud. "This all comes down to your masculine pride. Memphis's most eligible bachelor, unable to please his wife."

Show Adam the man who wouldn't take that as a challenge, and he'd show you someone truly pathetic. And they'd already established that wasn't him.

He advanced on her.

"Adam, put that knife down," Casey warned him, a wicked look in her eyes. He realized he was still carrying the butter-smeared implement, and tossed it onto the counter. She stepped backward, but soon came up against the fridge.

Adam put a hand on either side of her, effectively pinning her in position.

"I'll scream," she said. "The journalists outside will hear."

"I locked the gates last night," he reminded her. "There's no one here but you and your nasty husband."

He cut off her next words by pressing his mouth to hers. There was a moment of muffled protest, then the familiar heat rose between them and Casey was returning his kisses as fast as he could supply them. The tautness of her breasts through the thin cotton of her sundress, pressing against his chest, reminded Adam of that first day they'd met, when she'd run right into him.

She pulled away, but not before he'd completed a thorough exploration of her mouth. "Okay," she gasped. "I'll put out a statement to the media saying you're quite capable of satisfying me."

"But you don't know that," he said. "In fact, this whole thing with the housekeeper is your fault. If we'd been sleeping together—as I suggested," he pointed out virtuously, "she wouldn't have had any ammunition for her article."

"I'm not going to sleep with you just in case every housekeeper we hire turns out to be a spy."

"So much for your dedication to our cause," he said. "Let's get back to my strategy, since I at least am willing to prevent our good work so far from being ruined. I think Eloise is okay about these stories. I told her we were in separate bedrooms while the journalist was here because you moved out of our room in a fit of paranoid jealousy over one of my past relationships."

Casey squealed in outrage. "You and your ego. Why couldn't you be the one who was jealous about me?"

"Eloise knows I'm not the jealous type," he said smugly. "Let's not split hairs. We need to ramp up our marriage for everyone else to see."

"Ramp it up," she echoed.

"There's a charity gala on Thursday night," he

said. "I'm one of the patrons, so I'll be conspicuous. If you go with me, we'll both be conspicuous." She looked puzzled. "We'll be conspicuously happy."

"Okay…" she said doubtfully.

"And we'll invite your family to stay next weekend."

Casey groaned, knowing he was right. "I guess we should. Dad sounded suspicious about that article when he called yesterday, and I think he and Karen are making progress on getting their lives together. I wouldn't want to derail that."

She was struck with a brain wave. "How about we invite your family—all the stockholders in Carmichael Broadcasting—for lunch next Sunday?"

Adam looked less than enthusiastic about having to see his relatives on a weekend, but Casey persisted. "It can't hurt to mend some fences, Adam. Whatever the outcome of this court battle, you'll still have to work with Henry and Anna May. And if I introduce your family to mine, my folks will be even more convinced."

"That's not a bad idea," he conceded. "Maybe a barbecue. We can keep it casual."

"Sounds good."

"There's one more thing," Adam said. "We'll be sharing a room when your family is here. Don't you think it's time you and I made love?"

It was the first time he'd referred to it as "love,"

instead of sex or sleeping together. Casey sagged into her seat, put a hand to her stomach as if she could push down the heat that had pooled there. "Absolutely not," she managed to reply.

"It's going to happen, Casey," he said. "Start counting down."

ADAM HAD FLAT-OUT IGNORED Casey when she insisted she would buy her own clothes for the charity gala, and had sent Eloise to shepherd her around the best Memphis boutiques in search of the perfect dress. And what a dress it was.

The halter neckline of the lime-green satin gown flattered her bosom, the ankle-length slim skirt hugged her hips, and high-heeled black sandals gave her a seductive sway when she walked.

Not that Casey would be seducing anyone tonight, she told her reflection. But she wanted to look as if she was at least capable of seducing her husband. Adam's wasn't the only ego to have taken a hit with Saturday's newspaper article.

"You look great," Adam said when she met him downstairs. "How about you wear that on Saturday night?"

"Why on Saturday?"

"When we make love," he said, "I want to take that dress off you."

Her face flamed. "I told you, we are not going to make love."

He tsked. "Are you sure you're a pushover?" he said. "Because I'm not seeing it."

Casey beamed. He couldn't have paid her a nicer compliment.

Determined to defeat the gossipmongers, she held her head high and her husband's arm tight as she and Adam entered the restaurant for the gala.

There were probably a hundred and fifty people there, and Adam had to talk with many of them. Casey looked around for Eloise and found her in the middle of a group of elegantly dressed women.

"Casey, my dear." Eloise kissed her cheek, then introduced her to the others. It seemed Casey had interrupted a discussion about a controversial painting by Memphis artist Kevin Mallory, which had won a national award.

"It's gobbledygook," one woman said. "A mish-mash of colors, lines that go nowhere…what's it supposed to be?"

"It *is* mystifying," Eloise agreed. "But I find it not so much gobbledygook as—"

"Intriguing," said Sam Magill from behind her, once again startling Eloise. The women willingly widened their circle to include this unattached male. "I can't say I get what Mallory's trying to do, but you look at those colors—the depth—and it takes your breath away."

Sam had the women's rapt attention. He did look rather dashing, Eloise conceded, in a tuxedo that emphasized that he'd kept his shape. Really, some of those ladies were too silly, fluttering their eyelashes, flashing coy smiles that would have been more appropriate at a high school prom.

Eloise inched closer to him, in case the women were making him uncomfortable. But Sam didn't seem to mind the attention. He gave his views politely, allowed others to express theirs uninterrupted. That look of intelligent interest in his gray eyes was rather appealing….

Sam turned and caught her staring at him. His eyebrows rose a fraction. Eloise stepped away, and the movement drew his gaze to her new, high-heeled black sandals, which she knew flattered her ankles.

Sam's eyes lingered there a moment, then he said, "As always, you have excellent taste in shoes, Eloise."

She put her hands to her cheeks to cool the heat she could feel there, then turned to Casey. "My dear, you must let me introduce you to one of my dearest friends. Just over there…"

Casey managed to suppress a smile, but couldn't help shooting a look of encouragement at Sam as she was led away.

They hadn't gone far when Eloise stopped and gazed around the room.

"One of your dearest friends?" Casey prompted her.

Eloise blushed. "Perhaps I was mistaken. I don't see her now."

"We could go back to the others," Casey teased her.

"There's Adam's friend Dave Dubois, let's go and chat with him."

It was the first time Casey had seen Dave since he'd officiated at her wedding. She knew Adam had confided in him about the true state of their marriage, but he greeted her like an old friend, with an enthusiastic kiss on the cheek. Eloise got the same treatment. The older woman laughed, patted his hand, then had to excuse herself when someone summoned her.

"You look radiant," Dave told Casey, all extravagant charm.

"That sounded almost as convincing as your marriage celebrant impersonation."

He wagged a finger at her. "That was no impersonation, Mrs. Carmichael, and you have the husband to prove it."

"Thanks," she said dryly.

Dave inclined his head toward Adam, talking with the mayor of Memphis on the other side of the room. "He's more relaxed than I've seen him in a long time. I'd say marriage agrees with him."

Casey assessed Adam as objectively as she could. Dave was right. He smiled more these days, and he seemed less unyielding. "Maybe," she said.

"Does it suit you equally well?"

ABBY GAINES   197

She laughed at his blatant nosiness. "It suits both of us for a time."

"I don't know that you should be too hasty about ending it," he said. "Marrying you two…I couldn't have done better if I'd planned the whole thing."

"You didn't know that ceremony was for real, did you?" she demanded.

"No idea," he said. "But I've looked into it since—turns out, as an ex-commissioner, I can do all kinds of weird things."

Casey sipped her wine. "Can you issue annulments?"

"Uh, no." He shrugged in apology. "But if you want a permit to keep an alligator in your backyard…"

"Really?" She shuddered.

"Maybe I read that one wrong." Dave grinned. "It's mainly pretty boring stuff."

"Are you talking about a conversation with you?" Adam found the small of Casey's back, applied a pressure with his hand that moved her closer to him.

"I'm talking about what it must be like being married to you." Dave punched him lightly on the shoulder.

"Is marriage to me boring stuff?" Adam asked Casey.

The heat of his palm branded her back through the thin fabric of her dress. Somehow she'd moved even closer to him. If she stood on tiptoe her lips would brush his chin.

"Actually," she said, "it's kind of interesting."

For a moment, everything seemed suspended... her breathing, the chatter around them, the music... everything except the deepening intensity in Adam's eyes.

"If you guys don't quit ogling each other, I'm going to think there's more to this marriage than you both claim," Dave said.

Adam let go of Casey. "You'd be wrong." He glanced at his watch. "They'll be starting the speeches soon, I need to find out when I'm on."

He left, and Casey excused herself a minute later.

As the evening wore on, she found most people were interested to meet the woman who'd married Adam Carmichael on TV, but they were polite enough to keep a rein on their curiosity. Except for one man around her own age she could have sworn was flirting with her. He looked vaguely familiar.... Where had she seen him before?

She'd been fending off his advances for nearly ten minutes when he said, "I guess congratulations are in order. Maybe a Happy Anniversary?"

"Excuse me?"

"You've been married over a month now, haven't you?"

It was true. She and Adam had been married for

a month. Which meant any day now, the annulment would come through.

The stranger's words triggered the memory of where she'd seen him—below her bedroom window at seven o'clock on Saturday morning. This slug was a journalist. Casey struggled to keep her dawning realization from showing on her face. How could she use the knowledge to her advantage?

As it turned out, he handed her the opportunity on a plate. With what looked like deep concern, he expressed sympathy about the press coverage she and Adam had been subjected to.

She nodded gravely. "It was awful." She let a tremor enter her voice. "And all of it lies."

"Really?" He could barely contain his eagerness. "So you and Adam are, uh, a proper couple?"

With a naughty smile she said, "I don't know about proper." She leaned forward confidingly, and he did the same. "You've heard of spontaneous combustion?"

He nodded.

"Adam and I—we're like that." She winked, just to be sure he couldn't mistake her implication.

CHAPTER THIRTEEN

ADAM BROUGHT THE MAIL in with the newspaper at breakfast next morning.

He opened a lilac envelope without a stamp, hand-addressed to "Mr. and Mrs. A. Carmichael," and scanned the contents.

"Casey," he said silkily.

She looked up from her cereal. "Uh-huh?"

"This note is from Mr. and Mrs. Bob Harvey, saying they'll be delighted to attend lunch here on Tuesday.... Tell me it's come to the wrong address."

"Uh, not exactly," she said around a mouthful of cornflakes.

He scowled. "I distinctly remember telling you our marriage would be over if you invited the neighbors here."

"They brought flowers after those awful newspaper reports," she said. "This lunch is to thank them for their support. You'll be at work. You don't have to get involved."

"And it's just Mr. and Mrs. Harvey?" he asked suspiciously.

"Uh, I invited Alison Dare on the other side as well, with her three preschoolers. She and the Harveys don't know each other, but her kids don't have any grandparents, so I thought…"

With a snort of disbelief, he opened the newspaper and held it in front of his face. It was a milder response than Casey had expected. Relieved, she returned to her breakfast.

"What the—" He lowered the paper to gape at her. "Have you seen the headline on page five?"

"How could I when you're the one with the paper?" she demanded reasonably.

He turned it around for her to read, Casey Carmichael: My Husband's Hot. "Did you really say that?"

"Of course not. I told him *I* was hot." How could that idiot journalist have got the angle so wrong? And since when did she and Adam only rate as page five news? "Typical man, giving you the credit for any heat that's going."

"Entirely justified," he assured her. "As you'll find out very, very soon."

"I will not." Had he heard the waver in her voice?

ON SATURDAY MORNING, Adam proudly surveyed the Aston Martin's dazzling red bodywork. It was time consuming, but he still preferred to polish the car himself.

He just hoped he could do as good a job of convincing Casey's family to relinquish their demands on her. She owed it to herself to finish her book.

The other night, he'd asked if he could read some of her work.

"Writers don't let people read their stuff," she said. Then she handed him her almost completed manuscript.

Although Adam's teenage years were a distant blur, he was pretty sure he hadn't read anything this good back then. Casey had managed to capture teenage angst and put a comic spin on it. Adam figured her book might achieve the near impossible—getting young people not to take themselves so seriously.

He'd considered her novel-writing a silly dream. But Casey seemed to have a knack for making dreams come true.

When he heard the crunching of tires on gravel around the front of the house, Adam went inside and joined Casey at the front door to greet her relatives.

"Let's lay it on thick," he murmured in her ear—and got a jolt of pleasure at the wicked look in her eyes.

But they were only briefly arm in arm, presenting a united front. Then Casey rushed forward to take the baby, car seat and all, from Karen.

"Let me," she said.

Adam rolled his eyes and stepped forward. "Darling, that looks far too heavy for you," he said solicitously. He took the car seat from her and gazed down at Casey's niece.

"Isn't she gorgeous?" Casey demanded.

A far as Adam could tell, this was a pretty ordinary baby—red in the face, with a trail of drool at one corner of its mouth. He'd bet any daughter of Casey's would be far prettier. *Not that I care what Casey's babies might look like.*

"Gorgeous," he agreed with complete equanimity. He juggled the baby seat to shake hands with Casey's father, Ed, who in turn had to juggle the cane he was using to walk. Next, Adam kissed Karen on her cheek. Mike hadn't come, but since he wasn't the target of this campaign, that didn't matter.

When they got everyone inside, Adam had to forcibly restrain Casey from trying to simultaneously carry all the bags upstairs, make coffee and feed the baby its bottle. No wonder her family never did anything for themselves. He sent Casey and the others to the living room, put the kettle on the stove and took the suitcases himself.

He stowed Ed's in a downstairs bedroom, since the older man might have a problem climbing stairs. Karen's bag, along with the portable crib and a mini-Everest of baby gear, went in what was normally Casey's room. Leaving it there reminded Adam that he and Casey would be sharing a bed tonight. Not that he'd forgotten.

Tonight, he wouldn't take no for an answer.

Actually, he knew damn well that he would. Somehow Casey had ended up calling the shots on this sex thing. She was in control, and Adam hated it.

Yet somehow, he couldn't get mad about it.

Back in the living room, he walked right up to Casey and leaned over the sofa from behind to drop a kiss on the top of her head. "How are you, my love?" he asked tenderly. "Feeling better?"

"Is she ill?" Ed asked, confused. Casey looked equally puzzled.

"She's been working too hard," Adam said. "I'm always trying to get her to slow down."

"What work?" Karen said curiously. "The newspaper said you had a housekeeper."

"I'd never expect my wife to do housework, Karen." The guilt in her eyes suggested he'd hit the target. "Casey's been working hard on her writing," he elaborated.

It was plain from Karen's bewilderment that she'd never thought of her sister's writing as work.

"And you, Karen," he said. "You're not working at the moment, are you? You're taking maternity leave?"

"I—well, yes, but it's not easy looking after a baby on my own," she said, a tremor in her voice.

"That's right," Adam said innocently. "You wanted Casey to work as nanny for you, didn't you, so you could go back to your law job?"

If looks could kill, the daggers coming from Casey would have slain Adam on the spot.

Karen's lip quivered. "Casey always knows what to do. She'd be better with Rosie than I am."

"That's not true, honey," Casey assured her warmly. "Rosie's obviously very content—she's been asleep in her car seat ever since you arrived."

It was clear to Adam that Karen actually believed what she'd just said. So while she was being selfish in her expectations of Casey, that selfishness stemmed from fear, a lack of self-confidence. He figured that attacking her would only encourage Casey to take pity on her sister, which wouldn't be good for anyone.

So he said, "Of course it's not true. Babies take some getting used to, that's all. You'll be fine."

Smoothly, he steered the conversation to safer topics. He was still standing behind Casey, so he took the opportunity to give her a neck massage, as a loving husband might. Of course, it involved burying his fingers in that thick, lush hair to reach the tender skin of her nape. Barely discernibly, she arched against him.

He managed to keep his hands on Casey one way or another pretty much the whole afternoon.

"You're overdoing it," she said in a near whisper at one stage, when they were on the back veranda having predinner drinks. Casey had been sitting on the swing, cuddling the baby, her legs stretched out along the cushion. Adam sat on the end, and when she started to put her feet on the ground, he held on to them and played "This little piggy" with her toes—not saying the words, of course, but she knew what he was doing.

Did *he* know what he was doing? Other than having the time of his life? Of course he did. Play acting, that was all. Just enough to convince his in-laws he adored Casey.

Ugh. He was even thinking the word now. *It's only a word. Just because I'm thinking it doesn't mean it's for real.*

Still, Adam cooled it for a while, just stuck to the endearments and kept his hands off her. Which left him feeling as if his hands weren't doing what they'd been made for.

They had dinner late, after Rosie had been put to bed upstairs. During the meal, Karen revealed that she and her husband had now initiated divorce proceedings, so she was back in Parkvale for good. Adam learned that Ed had been doing poorly since Casey left. Both were feeling sorry for themselves, he surmised uncharitably.

At last Karen raised the hot topic of the week. "What about the article in last week's paper? It said you sleep in separate bedrooms."

"The woman was only with us a few days," Casey said. "Adam and I had an argument, so I slept in the guest room a couple of nights. It just happened to be while she was here."

"It was my paranoid jealousy," Adam said helpfully. Casey choked on her water. "Are you all right, darling?"

"Why were you jealous?" Karen asked.

"I found Casey flirting with the gardener," he improvised, and earned a hard kick under the table. "I mean, I *thought* she was flirting," he amended. "She wasn't, of course, and she moved out of our room until I saw sense."

Before he could get himself into more trouble, Adam raised his glass in a toast. "To the Greene family," he said, "who raised me the best wife a guy could have."

The others lifted their glasses, but when Adam sought Casey's eyes to share this moment of triumph, they were clouded with tears. Soon after dinner, she excused herself, saying she was tired and would go to bed. Had he done something wrong?

Adam was torn between wanting to go with her and the need to be courteous to their guests, to make amends for his earlier rudeness to Karen. He decided Casey would appreciate it more if he stayed with her family.

It was another hour before he made his own way upstairs.

The light was off, and he couldn't hear a sound. Could Casey have fallen asleep? When he knew he wouldn't sleep a wink with her beside him? Damn, she was annoying. In the darkness, he stepped carefully in the direction of the bathroom.

Casey closed her eyes when Adam switched on the light in the bathroom. She lay motionless until he'd closed the door. She'd never been good at hiding her feelings. What if Adam had already guessed the awful realization that had hit her this evening, after she'd endured a whole day of his caresses, his loving attention?

The realization that, for better or for worse, she was in love with her husband.

The knowledge weighed on her, holding her there.

Today's tantalizing glimpse of what it might be like to be truly married to Adam, if he loved her, had illuminated the truth she'd been denying for days. *This* was the meaning of the pleasure that curled in the pit of her stomach when he smiled at her. *This* was the cause of the physical ache his slightest touch induced. *This* was why, with him, she felt fully alive, one hundred percent herself.

All week, his assertion that tonight they would make love had caused excitement to thrum through her veins, heightening every sensation, invoking an unbearable tension, even as she'd told him it wasn't going to happen—and meant it. But now she knew she didn't have it in her to deny him.

Casey fidgeted under the crisp cotton sheets. Just knowing that his body normally occupied the space where she now lay was enough to set her on edge. She should have dressed, or rather undressed, for the occasion. Would Adam want her looking like this?

Would he want her if she told him she loved him?

The bathroom door opened, and Adam's deep voice called softly, "Here I come, *wife*."

"You're being Neanderthal again." Her attempt at a casual comment came out a squeak.

He chuckled, then the bathroom light clicked off, and she sensed rather than heard Adam making his way across the room in the dark. Casey froze, wondering where he would touch her first, the suspense tearing her apart. Where was he, dammit?

His hands brushed her collarbone as he reached for the duvet she'd pulled up to her neck despite the hot night. He tugged the cover away, and she felt the play of air over her body. Still he didn't touch her, yet she prickled all over. She heard the soft swish of the comforter hitting the floor, felt a sudden depression on the other side of the mattress. He was in bed with her, no more than a dark shape. She shouldn't have closed the shutters, not when she needed to see exactly where he was.

She felt his touch, featherlight on her forehead, smoothing her hair aside. He ran a finger down her nose, then traced the outline of her lips. Casey took his finger into her mouth, nipped the pad between her teeth, heard his ragged breath as she soothed it with her tongue.

He moved his hand to her nape, buried his fingers there the way he had earlier. Casey arched her neck, felt him shifting closer. When she lifted a tentative palm, she met the firm wall of his chest, felt the coarseness of the hair there. She wondered if he was already naked. Then she registered the brush of a silky fabric against her thigh. Boxers, she concluded.

His hands moved over her shoulders. Then he pulled away. "What on earth are you wearing?" The lamp on the nightstand snapped on, making her blink.

Adam stared down at her T-shirt and jogging shorts. Heat mingled with laughter in his gaze.

"You look fantastic," he breathed, and she giggled at the outright lie. The giggle turned into an indrawn breath as his hand caressed the bare skin of her abdomen where her T-shirt had ridden up.

"I guess your outfit means you're still not planning to let me make love to you," he said regretfully.

"Actually…" She licked her lips and saw his gaze follow the movement of her tongue. Her heart began thudding so strongly she thought Adam must surely hear. "It doesn't mean that at all."

He stared at her for a long moment. She nodded. A smile curved slowly across his lips and ended up in his eyes.

Then his mouth was on hers, and she was matching him, kiss for searing kiss. Whatever she'd said to that journalist about spontaneous combustion had been an understatement, Casey thought, as

Adam's lips trailed fire over her face, her neck and, nuzzling her T-shirt aside, her shoulders.

His hands roamed beneath the shirt, exploring the sensitized column of her spine, then moving around to cup her breasts. At that touch, Casey couldn't stifle a cry. Adam pulled away, breathing heavily. The need in his eyes was exhilarating…and terrifying.

"First," he said unevenly, "I need to get rid of your incredibly sexy nightwear."

He helped her tug the T-shirt off. For a moment, he held her hands over her head, snagged in the T-shirt, while he dipped his head to her breasts. She moaned and a low growl sounded in his throat. The T-shirt flew across the room. He reached for the waistband of her shorts and slid them down.

He paused, scanned her body with a heavy-lidded gaze that set her quivering.

"Your turn," she murmured, her hand fluttering toward his shorts in sudden nervousness. He peeled them off in one swift movement, and his glorious nakedness sent a charge of desire through Casey.

Adam touched a hand to her hip, then trailed a caress over her stomach, her breast, up her neck to her mouth.

She reached for him, and he shuddered, the guttural sound he made almost pained. He lowered himself over her so she could feel his hardness, feel how much he wanted her.

"My darling, you're so beautiful," he said.

She was ready for him right then. But the seduction he performed with his mouth, with his hands, was tantalizingly, achingly slow. He found every inch of her, bringing her to a level of desire she hadn't dreamed existed. And just when Casey thought she might die of it, he claimed her as his own.

CASEY AWOKE from the soundest sleep of her life to find herself alone in bed. She jolted upright, then relaxed again when she heard the shower running in the bathroom.

She lay there, hands splayed on the quilt, and let memories of the night before wash over her. The intimacy, the passion that she and Adam had shared had been beyond all her expectations. And despite her limited basis for comparison, it had been clear Adam found it equally sublime. Enough to want to repeat the experience twice during the night.

What next? Her body, which she'd believed to be sated, tingled in readiness. Not *that* kind of next, she told herself; what next as far as their marriage was concerned? She didn't expect Adam to have fallen in love with her overnight. But surely they'd moved onto a different plane.

The shower stopped, and Casey waited for him to appear.

To her disappointment, he emerged from the

bathroom fully dressed. Her cheerful greeting died on her lips, sent to its grave by the chill in his eyes.

"We need to talk," he said, and he sat on the very edge of the bed, leaving an expanse of quilt between them.

Casey waited, suddenly not trusting her voice. Adam seemed to have trouble finding the words he wanted, and for a few moments there was only a strained silence.

"Last night was a mistake. I know it was my idea, and I'd been pressuring you, but I was wrong."

"Why?" she managed to ask in a thin voice.

"I should have realized that because you were... less experienced, it would mean more to you."

"While it meant nothing to you?" she asked, stung.

His eyes darkened to indigo. "You know that's not true."

Maybe he was just worried for her, and she could reassure him. She reached across the coverlet and laid her hand on his.

He snatched it away as if burned. "Casey," he said, "last night was incredible. But it doesn't change anything between us. You and I still want very different things. You want a man who'll adore you. It's your dream, and it's what you deserve. But...I'm not the one who can do that. Making love—having sex—just confuses things."

Tears pricked her eyes, but she refused to cry. "You don't sound confused, and neither am I," she said over the lump in her throat. She steeled herself to lie to him, prayed she would be convincing. "I don't adore you, Adam, and I never thought you would be the man to adore me."

Was it relief that chased across his face?

"I didn't even take precautions that first time," he said. "You could get pregnant."

"It's most unlikely." Casey didn't bother to tell him why. There was hardly any point explaining her probable infertility when he'd just told her they had no future together.

Again he had the nerve to look relieved.

A surge of anger flowed through her, forcing back the heartbreak she knew would return later.

"Leave me alone, Adam," she said. "You were great in bed, but when it comes to relationships, you're a washout."

If she'd hoped he would protest, she was disappointed. He nodded, then left the room.

Casey heard him whistling on his way downstairs.

She eased back against the pillows, let out a slow breath, as if by making only the gentlest of movements she could somehow keep her heart from shattering. Just as carefully, she spread her fingers on the quilt again, forced herself to take another breath in and out. The dull gleam of the wedding ring on her left hand caught her eye.

She had more than this piece of jewelry in

common with Adam's mother. Like the woman who'd worn it before her, she had fallen in love with a husband who could never love her.

CHAPTER FOURTEEN

THE LAST THING Casey wanted was to face Anna May and Henry, along with the rest of Adam's extended family, for the lunch they'd planned. Why not just call an end to this charade now?

Because then Dad and Karen would know the truth. Because it would hurt Eloise, and Casey couldn't help wanting to postpone that moment. Because Adam needed more time to build his case against his father's will.

So they would go through with their performance.

Fortunately, both she and Adam were too busy getting ready for their guests to have any awkward moments together. Adam planned to barbecue, and Casey had a half-dozen salads to assemble, plus Eloise's favorite strawberry shortcake to bake.

By one o'clock, all the guests had arrived, and the beef fillet was grilling. Casey moved between the clusters of guests, introducing her family to Adam's, making sure everyone had someone to talk to and all glasses were filled.

Eloise watched her, proud of her gracious yet unaffected daughter-in-law. She knew something wasn't right between Casey and Adam, but she prayed that he would recognize Casey was nothing like his own family. That while she needed him, he needed her so much more.

Today, with the sun shining, and the sweet scent of magnolias mingling with grilling beef, it was easy to be optimistic. Eloise smiled as she turned back to her friends' conversation. But she had trouble focusing. Her mind was restless with thoughts of love and marriage. Unconditional love...

For some reason—probably because he was standing not twenty yards from her—Sam kept capturing her attention.

Adam should never have invited him to this lunch—he wasn't family. Of course, neither were Beth and Cecile. Adam had included them because he thought Eloise would prefer their company to some of his relatives'. It didn't help that Cecile kept giving Sam looks that could only be called flirtatious.

Somewhat acerbically, Eloise said to her friend, "You're rather obvious in your attentions toward Sam Magill, Cecile. It never pays to look too eager."

"It's called admiring the view," Cecile said promptly. "He's a handsome man."

"Tall, too," said Beth, who at five foot one said that about everyone. This time, Eloise happened to agree with her. "He keeps looking this way," her friend continued. "I think he's interested in you, Cecile."

Cecile straightened in her chair and sent a glance over her shoulder that Eloise considered far too sultry for a woman who'd turned sixty last birthday.

Eloise bit back the retort that it was *her* Sam couldn't keep his eyes off. Tears stung her eyes at the thought of how mean she was feeling toward her friend. What was wrong with her? With a huff of frustration that almost turned into a sob, she turned her back on Sam, trying for a joke. "You girls have been widows too long if you think Sam is anything other than a…a tedious, pathetic little man."

Oh dear, that hadn't come out funny in the least. She was met by horrified silence. Which was arguably an overreaction. She'd said no worse than the others had a dozen times about men who—

"Eloise." Sam's gravelly voice spoke behind her.

Eloise gasped. Her heart in her mouth, she turned. He seemed bigger than she remembered. Only a few inches taller than her five-seven, but just…bigger all over. Not overweight, just…big. Male.

She closed her eyes, mortified. Once, when she was a child, her mama had tanned her behind for being rude to one of their maids. And she'd been far less offensive then than she'd been to Sam now.

"Sam, I'm so very sorry. That was inexcusable." For the first time his gray eyes—gunmetal gray, she realized—didn't soften. This must be what he looked like in a courtroom.

He didn't blush or stammer or do any of the

inept Sam Magill things. "Eloise Carmichael," he said in the stentorian tone of a judge pronouncing sentence, "you are a spoiled brat."

Eloise heard Cecile titter, saw Beth's mouth round into an *O* of shock.

"When you decide to keep a civil tongue in your head like the lady you were raised to be…"

Oh, this was too much; now he was channeling her own thoughts back at her.

"…we'll talk about what you think of me. Until then, I'll leave you with this."

Strong hands grasped her shoulders, and Eloise looked up at him in bewilderment. A moment's stupidity prevented her from realizing what he was about to do. Then his lips met hers in a hard kiss.

She gasped and twisted away. "How dare—"

But his hands framed her face, forcing her back to him. Again he kissed her, smothering her protest with the hunger of a man too long denied.

Eloise pushed against his chest, but then— *gracious*—she seemed to be melting into the man. Her fingers curled into the fine linen of his shirt and she heard a noise that sounded very much like herself…*moaning*.

Finally, Sam released her, his face red, but not with embarrassment.

He cleared his throat and said stiffly, "I am not James. I will never be James." The words were a slap in the face. He took a step closer and Eloise shrank back even as a traitorous corner of her wanted to feel that mouth on hers again.

"You know what?" Sam said. "I don't *want* to be James."

He gave her that half bow, so much more awkward than James's had ever been, yet in its own way…endearing. Then he turned and strode across the lawn toward the drive.

On the way, he bumped into the sundial.

Eloise watched him until he disappeared from view. Cecile and Beth watched, too. Then Beth said, "You see, Eloise? I told you he likes you."

TO HER SURPRISE, Casey enjoyed the family lunch. Enjoyed being Adam's hostess, making his family welcome. Even Anna May and Henry. She especially enjoyed seeing Sam stake his claim to Eloise, who left soon after Sam did, pleading a headache.

Through the afternoon, Casey watched for an opportunity to speak to Adam's aunt alone. Casey hadn't discussed her plan with Adam. Now, she wondered if it was a dumb idea. Adam's family problems were none of her business, he'd made it clear this morning she was nothing more than a one-month wife.

But she loved him.

Her chance came when everyone had finished

eating. Most people sat around on the porch, nursing cups of coffee.

Adam, bless his orderly heart, was scraping down the barbecue and generally getting things straightened out.

Casey plunked herself down next to Anna May, who was watching Henry play tennis with some of his cousins on Adam's grass court.

"That boy is such an athlete," Anna May said fondly, before she realized who it was sitting next to her. She scowled.

"He's good," Casey agreed. To look at Henry's stocky figure, you'd never guess he was a sportsman. But he was wiping the floor with the admittedly limited competition.

"He's always been talented out on the court," Anna May said.

"As opposed to *in* court." Casey figured she might as well get right down to it.

Anna May glared. "I'm not talking to you without my lawyer."

"Anna May," Casey said. "Won't you consider dropping your legal action against James's will?"

Anna May sniffed. "Certainly. All Adam has to do is promote Henry and pay us a dividend. He owes us."

Casey drew a breath. This was where she either screwed up big time or pulled a rabbit out of the hat.

"I know you love Henry, and that's why you're fighting so hard on his behalf."

"Of course I love him."

"But Adam had the impression at one of your recent meetings that Henry's heart isn't in this battle."

The older woman blushed. "You don't know the first thing about what my son wants."

"I know what it is to do things for people out of love." She didn't say, *as a means of tying them to you.* "But in the end, it's not enough, for you or for them." She paused. "Have you asked Henry what he really wants?"

Anna May gaped. "Don't be impertinent. I know what my son wants. I know what I can do for him. Stay out of our business." She turned away to applaud, as Henry lobbed a killer serve that had his opponent scurrying for the ball.

Casey eyed the firm set of the other woman's shoulders with helpless frustration. She had been no help at all.

ADAM'S RELATIVES LEFT around four o'clock. With fewer people to act as a buffer, the strain between Casey and Adam became more apparent. They were wooden and stilted with each other, and despite Adam's best efforts, Casey found herself drifting into brooding silence.

She could barely hide her relief when her father and sister announced their imminent departure.

Before they left, Karen cornered Casey in the living room. "Have you and Adam had an argument? He puts on a polite front, but I can see you're both in a terrible mood."

Casey wasn't up to pretending any longer. "Yes, we have," she said simply.

"Are you certain you've done the right thing, Casey? I don't know how long you and Adam have known each other, but it can't be all that long a time. If this doesn't work out you can always come home to us." For once, Karen's concern sounded genuine.

"I don't know if my marriage will work out or not," Casey said. "Thanks for the offer, but I won't be coming back to Parkvale. I'm proud of you guys and how you're doing."

Despite this morning's disappointment, Casey knew an unfamiliar lightness of spirit. Finally, she'd said she wouldn't go back, and meant it. All those other times she'd talked about leaving home, she realized now, she hadn't been committed to building her own future. In getting away from Parkvale and writing her book, she'd discovered a kind of self-belief that all the affirmations in the world couldn't deliver.

Karen must have recognized the strength of her sister's resolve. "I'm sure we'll fix something up," she said meekly. She hugged Casey. "Good luck. Thanks for everything. And I do mean everything."

And that was it. Mission accomplished.

"YOUR WIFE WAS TELLING ME—" Sam's gaze slid away from Adam's "—I should show Eloise the real me."

"Casey said that?" Adam drummed his fingers on his desk. It was only Tuesday, but already he wanted this week to be over so he could spend two days with Casey. Which made no sense after what he'd said on Sunday.

"She's the only wife you have, isn't she? Or is this about to get more complicated?" The lawyer grinned. All through the meeting he'd been as chipper as Adam was sour.

Adam ignored Sam's joke. "If the way you groped Eloise in front of everyone was the real you, I'm not sure the world's ready for it."

Sam frowned and cleared his throat. "You may not have realized, but I am, er, very fond of Eloise."

"For Pete's sake, Sam, you all but ate her for lunch on Sunday," Adam snapped, not interested in hearing about other people's love lives when his own was such a mess.

Sam huffed. "I just want to warn you I intend to pursue Eloise with romantic intentions."

"Isn't she the one you should be warning? Assuming she hasn't figured it out already?"

"I intend to do that, too," Sam said.

"Okay, I consider myself warned." Adam let out a breath, and abandoned his churlish attitude. "Good luck with that."

The lawyer nodded, then switched the subject

smoothly. "Judge Skelton is back from vacation. I presented our annulment petition to him this morning."

Adam stilled. "Good." His voice sounded thin.

"If you're at all interested in making this marriage a permanent thing, I can ask him to hold off on his decision," Sam offered.

A rushing in Adam's ears left him dizzy. "There's no point," he said. "Even if Casey stays, Anna May told me she's going to argue in court that our marriage is fake, based on the TV wedding and the media coverage."

"I still think we can win our original argument that the will's not legal," Sam said. "What I'm saying is, if you and Casey do want to stay married, now's the time to say so. Then if Anna May gets somewhere with her new complaint, we can ask the court to allow a couple of years to demonstrate that your marriage is lasting and committed. If you and Casey stay married, we win no matter what."

"How do we prove our marriage is genuine, without inviting Anna May into our bedroom?"

Sam gnawed on his lip. "You have a baby."

A baby! Adam felt as if he'd been socked in the chest. He'd never thought about having children, but he did know he wasn't about to have a kid just to prove a point in court.

"It might be your best bet," Sam said. "We'll still challenge the will, saying your father can't force you to get married. But a lot of judges don't take kindly to that kind of thing. Most of them are within a decade or two of dying themselves. They don't like the idea of someone tampering with a man's final wishes."

"Casey and I aren't going to stay married." Adam was suddenly adamant on that point.

The decision weighed on him like a ton of that stodgy cornbread Eloise was so certain he liked. He looked at his watch. "It's nearly lunchtime. You must need a cigar by now."

The lawyer stood. "I've given them up."

Adam clamped his mouth shut to keep his jaw from dropping. "You love those things." Sam didn't smoke during working hours, but at the end of most evenings there were four or five cigar stubs in his ashtray.

Sam shrugged. "Eloise doesn't like it."

"Did she ask you to quit?"

"She's a lady, she'd never ask that. I wanted to do something for her."

Sam took his leave. Adam scowled at the door as it closed behind the lawyer. How did Eloise do that? Have men falling over themselves to do things for her without her having to ask? As far as Adam knew, she'd never asked anything of Sam. Adam realized now she'd probably never asked anything of his father, either. James had wanted to do things for his wife. Because he loved her.

"Love, schmove," Adam said.

He yielded to the irritation that had been pricking at him all morning. Instead of enjoying his work, all he could think about was his wife.

When had staying home with Casey started to outweigh the appeal of Carmichael Broadcasting?

Staring unseeing at his computer, Adam realized it was before Casey had spent last Saturday night in his arms. The tenderness, the passion of that night were symptoms of his current malaise, not the cause.

Which brought him to the real question: what exactly *was* this malady? There was only one diagnosis that didn't give Adam the urge to lock himself in his office and never come out again.

Lust.

That Casey occupied his thoughts to an alarming extent, not just with the memory of her exquisite body, but with her smile, her eyes, her laugh, her kindness, her mind. It all came down to lust.

He'd hurt her with his coldness the morning after they made love, he knew. But the generosity of her lovemaking had scared him. She'd given him everything, and that intimacy had been more precious than he'd known it could be.

Was she in love with him? Or did she at least think she was?

Adam told himself he hoped she meant what she'd said. That if on Saturday night she'd for some foolish reason thought she loved him, his coldness on Sunday morning had changed her mind.

Because Adam didn't do love. And he especially didn't do adoring.

He glanced at his desk calendar. If Sam's petition to Judge Skelton was successful, the annulment would be through very soon. Life would go back to normal. Adam forced himself to smile.

Hopefully, he and Casey could part as friends. Although, since Sunday morning, there hadn't been anything more than chilly politeness between them.

He should fix that before it was too late. Explain himself better, make sure she understood. And let her know he appreciated just how great her gift had been.

The clock on his wall clicked over to noon. That's right; she had the neighbors Adam had never met coming for lunch. At his house. With his wife.

"Cancel my afternoon appointments," Adam told his startled secretary. "I'm going home."

THE DOORBELL RANG at noon, just as Casey typed "The End" at the bottom of her manuscript. She'd written the book, she'd revised it to her satisfaction, and now those two little words gave her a deep feeling of accomplishment.

They also gave her a sense of foreboding. As if they might refer to more than her book.

She pushed her uneasiness aside as she went

downstairs, reminding herself to enjoy the release that came from not having an incomplete manuscript hanging over her head. *I feel great, really I do.* There was an almost genuine smile on her face as she pulled the heavy front door open to welcome the Harveys, and, coming up the walk behind them, Alison Dare and her children. "Come in," Casey said.

She'd just served the soup when Adam walked into the dining room.

What was he doing here? Surely he wouldn't throw the neighbors out, just because he'd told her not to invite them?

He walked up to her, kissed her lightly on the lips. "Hi."

"Hi," she said nervously.

Adam scanned the room. "Are you going to introduce me to your friends?"

Casey performed the introductions, then sat speechless through most of lunch as Adam chatted to Mr. and Mrs. Harvey about the changes in the neighborhood, and took an apparently genuine interest in Alison's three not-very-well-behaved children.

When Bob Harvey made mention of a street party as he left, Adam didn't even flinch.

"WHAT WAS THAT ABOUT?" she demanded, as he shut the door behind the departing guests.

He headed for his den, Casey on his heels. "What do you mean?"

"You didn't want them here. Why were you so nice?"

He leaned against the oak roll-top desk. "I know you could have coped on your own. But you shouldn't have to." When she didn't say anything, he added reluctantly, "That neighborly stuff matters to you. I thought you'd like it if I was here."

Casey caught her breath. "What do you care if I'd like it? You don't want me."

CHAPTER FIFTEEN

THE PAIN BEHIND HER WORDS seared Adam's conscience. "You can't seriously believe I don't want you."

"It's what you said."

And he'd been planning on saying the same thing to her again now.

They stood facing each other, a few feet apart, the tension almost a physical barrier between them.

Adam drew a calming breath, loosened the fists he'd clenched at his sides. "I care about you, Casey. That's why I came home. And I care about your future. You're a wonderful person—I hope you find a man who deserves you."

She took a step closer to him, then another, until she stood only inches away. She swallowed. "What if I find him and he doesn't want me?"

How, despite his best intentions, could Adam not reach out and pull her to him, kiss her hard on the mouth?

It took only a second of body-to-body contact for him to be on full alert and ready for a rerun of the other night. Casey's arms were around his neck, and she was kissing him with a fervor that left him in no doubt as to her wants. He ran his hands down her back to cup her derriere, pulling her against him, and she whimpered with need.

Clumsy with desire, he fumbled at the buttons of her shirt, at last managing to push the fabric aside to cup her breasts through the ivory satin of her bra. She arched against him, and he lowered his mouth to the swell of flesh. At the same time, he tugged the bottom of her shirt out of her shorts, slipped his hands inside her waistband. Suddenly, his progress eased considerably, and he realized she'd unsnapped her shorts. He slid them down and she stepped out of them. She began to tug at his belt.

Dimly, Adam registered that the phone on the desk was ringing.

He ignored it, concentrating instead on the incredible sensation of Casey's fingers undoing his trousers, then pushing them down. He kicked off his pants, then backed her toward the couch, not lifting his mouth from the tender hollow he'd discovered where her neck met her shoulder.

The room was silent, apart from muffled sounds of their need. So when Sam's voice boomed out from the answering machine, it was as if a bucket of cold Mississippi water landed on them.

"Adam, it's Sam. Good news, my friend. I had a call from Judge Skelton's office. He's granted your annulment. I'll send the paperwork out to you, but congratulations, you're Memphis's most eligible bachelor once again."

Adam would never have believed that *not* being married to Casey would be a complete passion killer. But it was. He no more wanted to make love to her now than she did to him—and he could see in her eyes that she'd gone right off the idea.

"We can't…" Casey choked on the words. She twisted from his embrace—he didn't try to stop her—and stumbled over to pick up her shorts, dragging them back on. Adam found his pants and dressed in silence, not trusting himself to speak for a moment.

"So that's it." Somehow he managed to sound calm, even casual, as he ran a hand through his hair to smooth it. "We got our annulment."

"I heard," she said shortly.

Already, there was a distance between them that was more than just the abrupt end to their love-making. Frustration and disappointment gnawed at Adam, and suddenly the room wasn't big enough for both of them. "I'm going for a run," he said.

AFTER HE'D RUN NEARLY three miles, Adam turned around and headed for home. Each thud of his shoes on the sidewalk hammered in the reminder that Casey would leave soon.

He didn't want her to go. She added an extra dimension to his life that he would miss. He could make her stay, of course. He sensed that if he wooed her, she could love him. She might even love him already. And marriage was in his long-term plan. So why not?

Because of the kind of marriage Casey wanted.

She wanted to be the most important thing in her husband's life. She'd never put it in those terms, but what else did being adored mean?

Adam breathed more heavily as he ran uphill. Only half a mile to go. *Think faster.*

He cared for Casey. He even loved her, in his own way. Though he wouldn't risk telling her that, in case she assumed he meant her kind of love. He wanted to be with her, he wanted to make love to her with a fierceness that scared him. He wanted to have children with her.

Never mind that until Sam mentioned it, he'd never thought about kids. Right now, something inside Adam went mushy at the prospect of a child of his own.

A son.

A chance for Adam to be the kind of dad his own father had never been.

A chance to heal some of the hurt of his youth, to set a new pattern for the Carmichael family. Adam snorted. Healing! He was starting to sound like Casey.

He rounded the corner onto his street. Home was just a couple of hundred yards away.

He forced himself to focus on the practicalities. As Sam said, having a child would prove their marriage was genuine. It could be the key to securing their future.

Adam wasn't prepared to trade his independence for the emotional ties he'd convinced himself Casey would demand. But maybe he was wrong about her. She'd changed in the past month, as he had. Her willingness to make love to him this evening, when she knew their relationship was nearing its end, when he'd reiterated they had no future, suggested a more practical attitude toward love.

Maybe he should lay his cards on the table, find out if his kind of love was enough to make a marriage work.

IT TOOK CASEY a few seconds to identify the source of the dread that enveloped her the moment she awoke the next day. She looked around her bedroom, with its luxurious furnishings, the wooden shutters at the window. This place had become home remarkably fast.

But no longer. There was nothing to keep her here.

She was thankful Sam's call had come before she and Adam made love again yesterday. How much harder today would have been! With the annulment, they'd tied up the last of the loose ends. The only remaining problem—Casey's broken heart—wasn't going to be fixed in a hurry. And it wasn't going to be fixed here.

She arrived downstairs for breakfast later than

normal and was surprised to find Adam still at the table, lost in contemplation.

He looked up at her and smiled, a movement of the mouth belied by the strain in his eyes. "Won't you join me?" he said, almost as if she were a stranger.

Casey tipped cereal into her bowl and nodded her thanks as Adam poured her a cup of hot tea. She ate in silence, aware of his somber scrutiny the whole time.

It was off-putting, and she pushed her bowl away when she was barely half-finished. The movement seemed to act as a cue.

"Can we talk?" he said.

"Of course." Were there more legalities to deal with?

Adam cleared his throat, and she realized he was nervous.

"This might sound odd," he said, "but now that we're no longer married…will you marry me?"

A bubble of hope, joy and laughter rose from deep within her, splitting her face in a grin. "Are you serious?"

Even as Casey asked, she realized Adam was extremely serious. In fact, he looked more as if he was about to have a tooth pulled rather than get married. And nothing like a man who had just realized he was in love. "Tell me more," she said with careful neutrality.

"It makes good sense," he said, and she had the

impression he was launching into a prepared argument. "We get along well, I enjoy spending time with you, we're physically compatible. You're a great wife, and I think you'd make a wonderful mother. We could remarry without anyone knowing we'd had our first marriage annulled."

"So it's convenient," she said. "And it fits nicely with your father's will."

He shook his head, seeming annoyed at her logical summation, even though it was just the sort of thing he would say himself. "I still believe I'll win in court, if that's all there is to it. But I'm very fond of you, Casey. We could make a good life together. *Very* fond."

Fond. That was how she'd felt about Joe. Five weeks ago, Casey had been prepared to give up on the idea of a man who adored her. Could what Adam offered be enough? Could she be satisfied with fondness on his part, and desperate, all-consuming love on hers?

"And Eloise loves you," he said.

Which only served to remind her that Adam didn't. And that Eloise had never given up on finding true love.

Casey added sugar to her tea, even though she preferred it unsweetened, and concentrated on stirring the gold liquid.

"We could have a baby," Adam said. "I know you'd like that."

Casey froze.

"Sam was saying a baby would help with our legal battle," he said. "He'll ask the court to delay its decision. He says the best way to prove our relationship is lasting and committed is to have a child." He paused, then a smile—a boyish grin—creased his face. He reached across the table, grabbed her hands. "A baby, Casey. Let's get married and have a baby."

Casey removed her hands from his. "Adam." Her voice shook. "I can't have children." And though she'd known it for a long time, telling him now brought a stab of pain so fresh it took her breath away.

It seemed a full minute before Adam spoke. "What do you mean—can't?" he asked, dazed.

Somehow she strung the words together. "When I had a perforated appendix as a teenager, I got an infection in my pelvis that damaged my reproductive system. The doctors tell me I'll never conceive." She pressed her lips together. "Does that answer your question?"

"Sweetheart, I'm so sorry." His tenderness was unexpected, and tears smarted in Casey's eyes. Adam came around the table and dropped down beside her. Gently, he pushed a strand of hair behind her ear, then ran a finger down her cheek. "My poor darling," he said, and her heart leaped. "I don't know what to say…."

Tell me you love me, that you want me for myself.

But she might as well wish for the problem with her fertility to magically disappear. Adam was being kind, but in his eyes she could still see shock and, worse, distance.

She looked at him steadily, made absolutely sure he understood what she was saying, and put the final nail in the coffin. "So if you want a child, it won't be with me."

She saw, in the sudden blankness of his expression, that he was letting her go. That although he wanted to marry her—and she knew, even if he didn't, that his offer included some degree of emotional commitment—he wanted to secure the business more. And she accepted that. He would never love her as much as she loved him, no matter how fond he was of her now.

He had made his choice; now she must make hers. So though it hurt beyond measure, she pushed her chair back and stood. "I'll leave tomorrow."

"Casey, there's no rush. Can't we—?"

"My writing conference starts tomorrow night," she reminded him. "It'll take all day to drive to Dallas." She paused. "I won't come back afterward."

Adam looked at her, stone-faced, and said nothing.

CASEY COULDN'T HAVE children!

Adam was still struggling to absorb it as he lay in bed, trying to sleep.

He felt betrayed, as if she had lied to him. He shouldn't, of course he shouldn't, but she'd allowed him to come to this momentous decision that he wanted to marry her, which went against all good sense, without telling him the one thing that would never have allowed him to get to this point.

He was being totally unreasonable, he knew. Hadn't he reiterated over and over to Casey that their marriage would have no future beyond the time it took to get an annulment? Until now, her fertility had been none of his business.

And yet he felt cheated of the babies he'd pictured them making together, robbed of the family life he'd imagined.

But however painful this was for him, it was worse for her. A part of him wanted to take her in his arms, comfort her, murmur to her that it didn't matter, they'd be all right.

But it did matter. And they wouldn't be all right.

CASEY DIDN'T SEE ADAM again until the next morning. She breakfasted early, alone, then went to pack her bags. She'd half hoped, half dreaded that he would go to work without saying goodbye, but when she came downstairs at nine o'clock, he was waiting.

"I'll take those." He picked up her bags and carried them outside, where he loaded them into the trunk of the Fiesta. It took only a minute, then she was ready to leave.

She cleared her throat. "Goodbye, Adam. It's been a memorable month. Thanks for your help." She stuck out a hand, but he ignored it.

Instead, he cupped her face in his palms and kissed her fiercely. "Goodbye, Casey."

She clambered into the car, holding herself rigid so she wouldn't cry. She turned the key in the ignition and—nothing happened. She tried again, several times. Still nothing.

"Aargh!" Casey thumped the steering wheel in frustration, and the movement released the tears she'd held in check for so long. She was weeping floods by the time Adam opened the door and helped her from the car.

He held her against him, arms wrapped around her, shushing her gently, one hand stroking her head.

"Don't cry, sweetheart," he said. "It's probably the battery."

"I got a new battery back in May."

"It'll be the starter motor then. We can have it fixed by tomorrow."

"But I have to be in Dallas tonight," she wailed, knowing she never would have cried about such a thing if she hadn't been at the end of her tether.

"Take my car."

She hiccupped. "I can't take the Aston Martin."

"Of course you can," he said calmly. He pulled his keys from his pocket and pressed the remote control.

The vehicle beeped obediently as the doors unlocked. "You have to get to Dallas and sell that book."

While Casey wiped her tears and blew her nose, Adam unloaded the bags from her trunk and put them in his. He handed her the keys. "Come back after the conference and we'll do a swap," he said. With sudden urgency he added, "Casey, I don't want us to part like this."

She summoned a faint smile as she thanked him for the keys and climbed into the car. But about their relationship, there was nothing left to say.

She drove off with a crunching of the unfamiliar stick shift that would have made a lesser man wince.

CHAPTER SIXTEEN

EVER SINCE CASEY HAD COME into his life, nothing had gone according to plan. Things hadn't gone wrong, exactly, Adam acknowledged, but if right meant "as planned," then they hadn't gone right, either.

It certainly wasn't right that he should be sitting in Casey's non-air-conditioned car in rush hour traffic on a stinking hot evening a week after she'd left. Why was he still driving this heap of scrap iron, of which the most valuable part was the new starter motor he'd bought earlier this week?

He could have taken a cab to the office each day. Instead, however unwillingly, he squeezed into the Fiesta and suffered the ignominy of being seen in a car sporting a Honk If You Think I'm Sexy bumper sticker, which had proven impossible to remove—and boy, had he tried. And all this because the car smelled, somehow, of Casey.

He scowled at the attractive woman in the BMW alongside, who had honked several times. That was another thing. There was no such thing as simple enjoyment of the opposite sex anymore. Adam used to admire the scenery as much as the next man, but these days, it seemed the sole purpose of the female species was to remind him of Casey.

If she and her pop psychology were right—that he was sublimating his wild side by driving an Aston Martin—what did it mean that he'd given her his precious car to drive? And that he hadn't worried about it while it was gone? Did that mean he was emasculated?

Don't go there.

Adam was only too aware that he teetered on the brink of something he'd assiduously avoided his whole life. At least, he hoped he was still on the brink—that he hadn't yet fallen in the kind of love that turned a guy's world upside down and clouded his logic. The kind that made him believe in preposterous happy endings that in reality just didn't happen. Or if they did they didn't last and you ended up like Eloise, fixated on the past. Surely it wasn't too late to get back to his orderly and—he was proud to admit it—predictable life?

Only it wasn't proving that easy. He'd been distracted in the office, impatient with his staff and less than polite to his stepmother. What really bugged him was that Eloise didn't even take offense, just smirked every time he grunted or snapped.

But what irked him most of all was Casey's parting gift. She'd phoned Mrs. Lowe and begged the housekeeper to come back to work for Adam.

And the grumpy old bat was driving him nuts. How could he ever have thought she was a treasure?

Casey's writing conference would be finished by now, and she should have returned his Aston Martin. But he didn't want to call her cell phone, for fear that, hearing her voice, he might give in to the seductive urge to stop obsessing about the business, remarry Casey and just enjoy life. Because what kind of sense did that make?

And Eloise had rolled her eyes when he'd asked her to help get his car back, even though he knew she was still in contact with Casey.

He needed a distraction from his distraction. There was probably a psychological term for it; he must ask—

Cancel that.

By the time he got home, Adam was hot, uncomfortable and sick of being honked at. Did the women of Memphis have nothing better to do? In a fit of pique, he hurled Casey's car keys into the garden, where they sank out of sight into a yew hedge. Ha! Temptation removed. Now he'd have no choice but to take a cab to work.

Pleased that he'd taken the first step toward banishing Casey from his head, Adam checked the answering machine. Instead of deleting all the messages from women who'd called to tell him how sorry they were to read of his annulment in the newspaper this week, he called a couple back and arranged to meet for a drink over the next few evenings. No more sitting around the empty house.

And he'd better sort out his costume for Eloise's birthday party, which was a masked ball in the traditional style of her youth. The party wasn't for a couple of months, but it didn't hurt to be prepared.

Adam whistled cheerfully as he signed on to the Internet and began surfing the Web sites of costume shops. It was a good five minutes before he realized he was whistling "You Are My Sunshine."

Two months later

"YOU MUST HAVE SOMETHING more affirming," Casey pleaded down the line to the help desk at the phone company. "You Are My Sunshine" simply wasn't powerful enough to counteract the funk she'd slid into since the annulment.

"How about 'Blue Eyes' by Elton John?" the girl on the other end suggested.

"No!" Casey took a deep breath. "Do you have that old Split Enz tune 'I Hope I Never Have to See You Again'?"

"It doesn't sound very affirming," she said doubtfully, "but I'll check."

They didn't have it, and Casey ended up settling for "Love Is a Battlefield." She gave her credit card number and got the code to download the new ring tone. She'd barely finished the process when her phone rang.

"Eloise." She greeted the older woman with genuine pleasure. "How are you?"

Eloise had called to remind her Casey had agreed to dine with her tonight. "I can't wait to see you, dear," she said. "It seems so long since we had a good chat."

Guilt pricked at Casey. She'd been so busy working on her new book that she frequently lost track of time, shut away in the studio apartment she'd leased near the center of Memphis. In the evenings and on weekends, she was tutoring several kids in English. She hadn't had much time for Eloise.

"I'm looking forward to it," she said. She ended the call, pleased she'd stuck to her resolution of not asking Eloise about Adam.

Not that she needed to ask. She'd never heard of Adam Carmichael before she married him, but now she couldn't escape him. In the first few weeks after their annulment, which had been front-page news for only one day, his name had appeared regularly in the business section, or in support of some charity. She shuddered as she recalled the photo she'd seen of him with a gorgeous, dark-haired woman on his arm.

Casey didn't want to know how Adam was getting along without her. It was easier to quit reading the newspaper. Besides, she was too busy to keep up with the Memphis gossip. She had sold her first book—an editor from the conference had picked it up—and Casey was making progress on her second.

She went back to Parkvale most Sundays to visit Karen and the baby. She didn't usually see her dad, because he'd started dating a woman in the next town and had taken up driving again.

On the subject of driving… Casey peered over her computer screen to a window of her apartment, and checked that Adam's car was still parked in the street below. She was terrified it would be stolen, yet couldn't bring herself to return it to him. She'd hoped it would bring him back to her, however briefly. But it seemed Adam was willing to relinquish his beloved car rather than speak to Casey again.

She sighed. What was the point of postponing the inevitable? She would leave the Aston Martin at Eloise's tonight and take the bus home. Adam could get the Fiesta back to her however he chose. She would take the car for one last spin, to lunch with Brodie-Ann, who'd taken a day off work and should arrive in Memphis any minute.

When Brodie-Ann arrived, they drove to the park.

"You sure get a lot of attention in this car," her friend commented, as yet another man honked his horn at Casey, then gave her a thumbs-up when she looked in her rearview mirror.

"I don't miss my Honk If You Think I'm Sexy bumper sticker," Casey agreed as she gunned the engine and took off from the lights, leaving the car's latest admirer to eat her dust. She'd attracted more male attention in the past two months than she had in the previous twenty-five years. She would miss roaring around town in this beast.

Not that she needed the car as an ego boost. She'd had plenty of offers of dates, from men who hadn't even seen the Aston Martin. No, these days her confidence ran deeper than affirmations, deeper than how many men asked her out, deeper than the dubious satisfaction that came with believing others couldn't cope without her.

Thanks to Adam.

In the time she'd spent with him—and, ironically, through the inept marriage proposal that had ended their relationship—he'd taught her she could survive, and thrive, without being someone else's crutch. That life's rewards were about taking as well as about giving. That settling for what she could get wouldn't make her happy, but following her passion would. Things she'd suspected before, but never had the courage to test.

When they arrived at the park, Casey and Brodie-Ann sprawled on the grass with their picnic lunch. It was a bittersweet reminder of that picnic Casey and Adam had enjoyed. And it was only a hop, skip and a jump from there to thinking about the one night they'd spent together. Casey had half hoped that, against all odds, she might have conceived Adam's child that night.

She hadn't.

So here she was, oozing misery, while Brodie-Ann couldn't stop chirping about how wonderful Steve was, how incredible married life was. Her friend tapped her soda bottle against Casey's in a toast. "Here's to three months of wedded bliss."

"Happy anniversary," Casey said gloomily.

"You were right. Steve and I are made for each other." Brodie-Ann grinned. "Things have been great since I figured out how that give-and-take stuff works."

She scrutinized Casey. "Speaking of give and take, have you seen Adam lately? As in, he gave you his Aston Martin and you took it?"

Casey shook her head. "I keep thinking he'll come and demand it back."

She didn't state the obvious. That Adam was so anxious to avoid her, not even his precious car would bring him to her.

Brodie-Ann patted her shoulder. "You're doing great, Casey. Hang in there."

Casey nodded. Things *were* good. She told herself that every day. She had a book contract; she was getting by. And she no longer depended on people being unable to cope without her.

The only goal she'd failed to achieve was the no-strings love. Because Adam had come with as many strings as every other person Casey loved.

AT SIX O'CLOCK, Casey drove to Eloise's house. She climbed out of the Aston Martin and locked it for the last time, then mounted the steps to the porch.

Eloise opened the front door.

"Come in, dear." She tugged Casey inside, then quickly shut the door behind her.

"Is something wrong?" Casey looked around. "Eloise, what's going on?"

The foyer was festooned with streamers and flowers. A uniformed waiter hurried past her carrying a silver tray stacked with wineglasses. Down the wide corridor to the back of the house, Casey could see doors flung wide to the garden and—was that a marquee?

"Eloise, tell me."

The older woman's eyes danced above her guilty smile. "Just a little party, dearest. For my birthday."

"A *little* party?"

"Fewer than three hundred guests, I promise you. Much smaller than last year." She took her hand. "I'm sorry, Casey. I so wanted you to be here, and thought you wouldn't come if I told you."

"I suppose Adam's coming?" Casey grumbled.

"Of course. He hasn't been happy lately, and I thought a party might cheer him up." Eloise's eyes didn't meet Casey's as she added, "I don't recall if I told him you'd be here."

Casey shook her head, indicating any attempt to match her and Adam up again would be futile, but didn't comment. Eloise knew as well as she did that a party was the last thing Adam would want if he was under stress. Casey told herself that why he wasn't looking happy wasn't her business. He probably missed his car.

She glanced down at her slightly rumpled cotton shift. It had seemed all right for a casual dinner with Eloise. "I'm not dressed for a party."

Eloise accepted that as agreement that Casey would stay. She smiled as she squeezed Casey's fingers. "I know, dear, and I hope you won't mind that I took the liberty of buying you something. A birthday present from me to you."

Casey couldn't help laughing. "Shouldn't it be the other way around?" She allowed Eloise to lead her upstairs to a guest bedroom.

"Oh." She was left almost speechless by the dress she found there—a strapless, midnight-blue silk creation that she knew just by looking would fit perfectly. And it did, hugging her curves as if made for her.

"My hairdresser is waiting to do your hair," Eloise said. "And I bought you this." From a box on the bed she lifted out a mask, elaborately decorated with gold feathers and blue ribbons.

"It's a masked ball, darling," she said, seeing Casey's confusion.

A sinking sensation hit Casey. Surely Eloise

wouldn't… "Tell me this isn't a bridefest," she demanded.

Eloise snickered. "That's a one-sided way of looking at it. There are several very eligible men coming tonight. Think of it as a groomfest."

"YOU WIN, CASEY."

Alone in the silence of his office, Adam found the words easier to say than he'd expected. Instead of feeling as if he'd lost control, anticipation thrummed through his veins. Anything might be possible when he had Casey by his side….

Except she wasn't by his side. Because he had let her go.

Smart, Adam. Very smart.

He tucked the phone between shoulder and chin so he could lift a sleeve and look at his watch. Seven o'clock. His stepmother's party would be starting right about now. He didn't want to go—he didn't want to go anywhere ever again—without Casey.

"Did you say something?" Sam had been hemming and hawing on the other end of the line as he shuffled through his papers, searching for the relevant section to read to him.

Adam shook his head, though of course Sam couldn't see that. "Just thinking aloud," he said. He could picture the lawyer pursing his lips.

"Strikes me you've done too much thinking lately," Sam muttered. "This was one crazy idea.

I'm amazed the judge even agreed to it. Wouldn't you be better just to move on?"

Adam grinned, ridiculously light-headed. "That's your professional opinion, is it?"

"For what it's worth." Sam clearly doubted his advice would be followed. "Still, what's done is done. Just don't expect to be able to undo it so easily."

"I won't be undoing it," Adam said confidently. He leaned back in his chair, propping his feet up on his desk in a way he never did. "Are you going to Eloise's party?"

There was a pause at the other end. "She didn't invite me. Which in itself is significant, don't you think?"

"Uh, maybe," Adam said.

"I'm going anyway."

"You're gate crashing?" Sam never did things like that. No one did things like that to Eloise.

"I believe that is the vernacular term for it," Sam said stuffily.

"Wow." Adam was impressed. "I guess I'll see you there."

He ended the call and changed into the tuxedo he planned to wear. But instead of heading to Eloise's house, he drove the company car he was using, while he figured out what to do about the Aston Martin, toward the leafy suburb where Casey had her studio apartment.

Repeatedly pressing her doorbell brought no

response. Adam cursed. He'd been so buoyed up by the thought of seeing her, by what he had to tell her, he could hardly believe she wasn't at home. No sign of her car—his car—either.

He would wait.

CHAPTER SEVENTEEN

SAM CLAMBERED OUT OF the taxi at Eloise's house, then took a moment to adjust his costume. Damned uncomfortable getup. The breeches were tight enough to pose a permanent risk to a man's ability to demonstrate his passion, the coat sleeves ended in a froth of lace around his wrists, and as for the color… Sam had never worn peacock-blue in his life and, after tonight, he never would again. He'd drawn the line at the wig. He was Prince Charming, not Prince Ridiculous.

He looked at his watch through the slits in his mask. Eight-thirty. The party would be in full swing. He would make a dramatic entrance, say his piece, claim his prize. Then endure a few more hours in this costume.

He picked up the cushion he'd placed on the step while he straightened his outfit. It took two hands to carry the blasted thing; the glass slipper was attached by discreet threads, but wobbled unromantically if he didn't grip it right.

Sam blew out a calming breath. Wearing this

silly costume was a small price to pay if he got what he wanted. He reminded himself how Eloise had responded to his kiss at that barbecue lunch—she'd been even more shocked than he was at her passion. He didn't doubt that was why she hadn't invited him tonight. She was running scared, though she might not know it.

In his younger days, Sam had worked as a prosecutor of white-collar criminals. Some of his most satisfying moments had come from cases where a key witness hadn't been able to see what had been right there all along. When awareness dawned, the witness's credibility was even greater than that of one who'd told the same story right through. That was when Sam knew he had the case in the bag.

He paused at Eloise's front door. He wouldn't go so far as to say he had Eloise in the bag. But she was in that dawning realization phase. And because Sam was several steps ahead of her, he had the upper hand.

He lifted the heavy brass knocker, and let it fall with a thud. Instantly, the door was opened by a man in uniform, whose eyebrows shot up.

Sam stepped inside.

And realized immediately the advantage an invitation would have given him.

"So," he said to the doorman, as he surveyed the sea of women dressed in bright evening gowns and tuxedo-clad men, "it's not a fancy-dress ball, then?"

"No," the man agreed. "Just masked."

Sam sent up a brief prayer of thanks that he'd resisted the suggestion of the girl in the costume shop that he paint an authentic eighteenth-century beauty spot on his cheek.

"Sir, do you have an invitation?" the doorman asked.

Sam decided he'd had enough of chatting to the hired help. He'd screwed up on the costume front, but he still had his mission. Clutching his cushion and glass slipper, he stepped forward and paused in the entryway, scanning the crowd for Eloise.

"Hey!" the doorman called from behind him, but Sam ignored him.

There she was, stunning in dark green velvet, a dress that molded her slim waist and showed she had enough curves to satisfy any man. Her gold-and-green mask rendered her mysterious, exotic, but still the Eloise he…loved. Yes, loved, dammit.

He'd behaved like an idiotic schoolboy the past three years. But over that time, his feelings for Eloise had grown into an unshakeable love. If she wouldn't have him…

Her eyes met his across the room. He imagined them widening with shock beneath her mask, as much that he'd dared to arrive uninvited as with surprise at his costume. She raised her hand to her lips, but Sam saw the corners of her mouth quirk. She was laughing at him.

Declaring his love for her now would doubtless send her into hysterics.

Sam tasted bitter disappointment, and swallowed. So the witness hadn't yet reached the stage of enlightenment that he'd hoped. It was his job to fix that.

He nodded curtly to Eloise, shook off the restraining hand of the doorman, then strode into the crowd, away from her.

ADAM WAITED OUTSIDE Casey's apartment until eleven o'clock, growing increasingly despondent, then annoyed.

She'd better not be out on a date.

He pushed away the unreasonable jealousy that thought provoked. He wanted to see Casey tonight, but had to accept that might not happen. The evening might be a disaster for him, but he'd better not disappoint Eloise by missing her birthday party.

When Adam pulled into Eloise's driveway, things started to look a whole lot better. In the glow of the fairy lights threaded around the pillars on the porch, he saw his Aston Martin sitting right by the front door.

Elated, he ran up the steps and into the house. People thronged the foyer, the staircase, every available space to the marquee out the back. Adam made his way toward the ballroom.

He saw her immediately. Casey, in the arms of a man he didn't recognize. But he did recognize the sappy smile the guy was giving her.

As Adam watched, the man leaned close and whispered something in Casey's ear. Adam stiffened, his hands clenched at his sides.

At a light touch on his arm, he turned. It was Eloise, resplendent in dark green velvet and a green-and-gold mask.

"Adam, darling." She patted his cheek below the blue domino mask that didn't hide his identity one bit. "You made it."

"I'm sorry I'm late," he said formally, his gaze back on Casey, who appeared to be smiling at something that jerk had said.

"You've been unbearably slow these past months, but you're not too late, and that's all that matters."

"Huh?" Adam turned back to Eloise, who was also looking at Casey. Of course, his stepmother had known she would be here tonight, but had chosen not to mention it to Adam. No doubt part of some elaborate scheme to bring them together.

Typical. Didn't she know he had this all mapped out?

But gratitude for her good intentions welled in his heart, constricting his chest. "Thanks," he said gruffly.

Eloise smiled at him, tears in her eyes. "Go," she ordered. "Claim your bride, before Richard Lovington III nibbles her ear off."

Further realization dawned, halting Adam in his steps. "Your birthday's not till November," he accused her. "This party isn't for you. It's for me—and Casey."

Eloise sighed, but the look in her eyes was far from penitent. "It's the bridefest, darling. I know I shouldn't have, but I—"

Adam hushed her with a kiss on the cheek. "Thank you," he said again. "Thank you, Eloise."

She hugged him, then pushed him away, brushing impatiently at her eyes. "I don't think I'll ever understand men," she said. Half indignant, half amused, she added, "Sam came to my party without an invitation. Look at him!"

Adam choked on a laugh. The preposterous elegance of Sam's Prince Charming costume couldn't hide his distinctive shuffling step, even as he danced with a woman in a low-cut red dress. "Has Sam danced with you?" he asked.

"He hasn't even spoken to me," Eloise huffed. "What does the man think he's playing at?"

The dance ended, and as if he'd guessed the subject of their conversation, Sam made his way over to Adam and Eloise.

The two men nodded to each other. Adam swallowed his comment about Sam's outfit.

"Good evening, Eloise," Sam said. He stood close to her, and Adam saw that she didn't move away, but swayed toward him slightly.

"Sam." Her voice was cool.

"It seems my invitation to your party went astray," he said.

"I didn't send you one."

"Then I apologize if my presence here embarrasses you."

Eloise inclined her head. "Not at all."

"I had to come," Sam said.

"To check how I'm spending my money?" Eloise asked. "To see if I've briefed the catering staff correctly? To nag me about keeping my insurance paid up?"

"To dance with you," Sam said.

"Oh." Eloise was clearly flustered.

Adam enjoyed the spectacle.

But she had no trouble seizing the upper hand again. "Then why haven't you asked me to dance?" she demanded acerbically.

"I've been waiting for the band to play the tune I requested." Sam paused, alert. "It should be about now."

Sam had done it again, Adam realized. Knocked Eloise off balance. For the first time, it occurred to him the lawyer might be good for his stepmother.

The band struck up "All the Things You Are."

Eloise caught her breath, glanced uncertainly at Adam. He nodded encouragement. She turned to Sam. He gave her his hand. "Dance with me."

CASEY HAD LOST COUNT OF the men she had chatted with over dinner in the marquee, and danced with in Eloise's ballroom. But despite the masks that concealed their faces, she knew none of them was

Adam. Had he heard she was coming and decided to stay away? Eloise was at a loss to explain his absence, and Casey sensed the older woman's disappointment. Damn the man.

Then, as if her anger had conjured him up, he appeared over the shoulder of her current dance partner, masked but instantly recognizable.

Adam tapped the other man on the shoulder. "May I?"

Her partner, who had been in the middle of asking her out to dinner, hesitated. To Casey's shock, the infallibly polite Adam Carmichael elbowed him out of the way. The other man started to say something along the lines of "See you later," but the glitter in Adam's eyes, behind his blue domino mask, deterred him from finishing.

Casey fitted her hand into Adam's, trying to calm the sudden racing of her pulse. How had he recognized her in a dress he'd never seen, with a mask obscuring most of her face and hair?

But she said nothing, just relished the sensation of his hand at her waist. For a few moments they danced in silence.

"I knew you by your shoulders," he said at last, sounding almost angry.

"I…what?"

He lifted his hand and ran a finger along her shoulder, from her neck to the top of her arm. Casey shivered.

"Isn't that curious?" he said, his tone conversational now. "I walked into the room and I knew you."

"Curious," she agreed, hardly daring to breathe.

He pulled her closer, both hands on her waist as they danced. Casey was faint with desire.

"I've been reading about you in the newspaper," she said.

"That photo. That woman?" he asked, and she nodded.

"There's a psychological term for it," he said. "Sublimation, or substitution—something like that."

"Substitution for what?"

"You're the psychologist, you figure it out. But know this—I haven't so much as touched another woman since you left. Not beyond a kiss on the cheek."

"Thank you…." But it wasn't enough. "It's been two months."

"Some people are slow learners." He rested his chin lightly on the top of her head. "I have some bad news for you."

"What's that?"

"I had your car towed away."

"You what?" Casey pulled back in alarm, but he wouldn't let her move more than a couple of inches.

"I lost the keys," he said. "What else could I do?" He'd maneuvered her to the doorway that led to the back porch, and they stepped out into the cool evening air. He guided her to a seat on the edge of the porch, where he pulled off his mask and, without speaking, helped Casey remove hers.

"So I want you to keep the Aston Martin," he continued.

She gaped. "But you love that car."

"It's not a car, it's the sublimation of my boy-hood dreams." He smiled, took both her hands loosely in his own. "I have different dreams now."

"Which are?"

"I'll get to those in a moment. Besides, I wasn't happy at the thought of my wife driving around in that heap of rust you call a car."

"I'm not your wife."

"Ah, yes. That's the other piece of bad news. We're still married."

Her heart stopped for a moment. "What? How?"

"All my fault, I'm afraid." He didn't look the least bit apologetic. In fact, she'd bet he was enjoying her outrage. "I couldn't live a lie any longer."

"What lie? Adam, what is this?"

"Sam gave me a copy of the judgment from our annulment hearing. Turns out the judge considered two key factors in deciding to grant it. First, we hadn't intended to get married. And second, we hadn't—"

"Consummated the marriage," she finished for him. "Oh, no."

"That's not a particularly flattering reference to our consummation," he said.

"So this is about your ego? You didn't want it on public record that you hadn't slept with your wife?"

He tightened his grip on her hands. "It wasn't public record," he said. "The judgment was sealed. I petitioned the court to revoke the annulment because I couldn't bring myself to deny the best night of my life."

"The best?" Casey swallowed.

He nodded. "Sam argued the case at the county court, and he called me earlier tonight to say the judge revoked the annulment."

"So now what? We get divorced?"

"Now, I tell you my new dream. Which is to spend the rest of my life being distracted, provoked and seduced by you."

"You asked me to marry you once before, Adam, and I told you no."

"But this time I'm laying down some strict conditions," he said.

"Oh, are you?" Indignation colored her tone.

"You might think it's okay to be fond of your husband, but I'm settling for nothing less than mutual adoration." He lifted her fingers to his lips and kissed them.

The reminder of the day they'd first met, when he'd told her she might never find a man who adored her, brought a lump to her throat. Casey gazed into his eyes, and saw all she needed to know about how he felt toward her.

"Adoration? That's a lot to ask," she said thoughtfully. "You could wait a long time for a woman who adores you, Adam. You might never find one."

"I'll wait," he said.

"But what about your father's will? What about that baby you want to have, to secure the business?"

"That's all over," he said. "Soon after you left, Anna May backed down from her lawsuit. Turned out Henry didn't really want to run the company. He wants to coach high school tennis and still pick up a fat dividend from the business every so often. I said that can be arranged."

"That's great."

"Anna May figured all this out after you gave her a lecture about wanting what's best for the people you love," Adam told her. "She asked Henry and he finally got up the guts to tell her what he *did* want."

He broke off as another couple stepped out on the porch. A loaded stare from Adam soon had them retreating back into the ballroom. "Once Anna May dropped her opposition, Sam was able to get the marriage clause struck from Dad's will."

"So you don't need a wife," Casey said. "Or a baby."

Adam squeezed her fingers. "But I do need *you*. I need your company, your love, your faith in me, the way you inspire me to be a better person."

"What about a baby?" Casey asked. "Because if you need one of those…"

"We'll figure something out," he said carelessly.

"No!" She stood and stepped back.

He rose to join her, his face pale. "No, you won't stay with me?"

"Adam, I love you—I adore you—and I want to us to be married. But I can't promise you a baby."

"We'll figure something out," he told her again. "Maybe, if you want a child as much as I do, we could look at adopting. I know you'll be a great mom, whether it's our natural child or not. Or if you want, we can try for our own baby and decide that whatever will be, will be."

He leaned forward and kissed her gently. "I adore you, my precious, darling wife. Stay with me forever, and we'll take everything else as it comes."

Had there ever been as sweet a sensation as this? Casey almost laughed out loud with sheer joy.

"If I say no, do I still get to keep the Aston Martin?"

He chuckled. "Of course."

"Mrs. Lowe's not going to like it if I come back," she warned him. "You'd better think hard about this, Adam, because it's her or me."

"I've already sent her off into retirement with a healthy bonus," he said. "I couldn't take another day of those frosty grimaces she seems to think are smiles."

Casey giggled, then snuggled into his embrace. "I was wrong about something," she said against his chest.

Adam kissed her hair. "You, darling? Never."

She pulled away just a little. "I agreed when you said we should be selfish. I said I wanted no-strings love. But it's not true. I want to be tied to you, Adam. And I want you tied to me."

His eyes, brilliant with emotion, met hers. "Real love," he said, "comes with strings you tie yourself."

Casey's heart swelled. The man was the perfect soul mate for her. It seemed too wonderful to be true. Reluctantly, she came back to the stumbling block she couldn't believe might not prove impassable. "You're sure you don't mind if we never have our own baby? I wouldn't blame you if you did."

He paused. "Of course I want you to have my child. But Casey, you are the only woman for me, baby or no baby."

She planted a kiss on his chin. "And what about—?"

"Enough," he ordered. "You can make as many objections as you like, but I'm not going to change my mind. I adore you, you're my wife and we have the rest of our lives to argue over the details. Now, are you coming back to me or not?"

"Of course I am."

The kiss that followed lasted a very long time. When they parted, Adam's eyes were dark with desire.

"You're quite sure we're still married?" Casey asked.

"Positive."

She held out her hand to him. "Then I know just what I want to do next."

They pushed through the throng, hand in hand, single-minded in their determination to reach one of Eloise's many bedrooms. But Casey stopped dead when she heard "All You Need Is Love" playing tinnily from the vicinity of Adam's pocket.

She turned to grab him by the lapels. "What," she demanded, "is that?"

Sheepishly, Adam pulled out his cell phone. "Personalized ring tone," he said. "It's affirming."

Casey took it from him, pressed the off button, then slipped the phone back into his pocket. On tiptoe, she pressed her lips to her husband's. "Stick with me," she said, "and I'll give you all the affirmation you'll ever need."

EPILOGUE

"SHE LOOKS NOTHING LIKE her cousin." Casey placed their beautiful daughter back in her crib and tucked the blankets around her tiny body.

"She's way more beautiful." Adam leaned forward to get another good look at his second-best girl. "This one takes after her mom."

"She's very noisy," Casey agreed with a grin. "And she likes fast cars."

"And she's worth any amount of effort," Adam said, conscious that most of the effort had been Casey's. She'd had to have the surgery to repair her damaged fallopian tubes twice before it worked. But for the rest of their lives, Adam would do whatever it took to cherish his family. Casey nodded, tears glistening in her eyes. She always insisted her out-of-kilter hormones were responsible for her easy tears, but Adam knew his sensitive wife better than that.

He continued to list the similarities between his daughter and his wife. "And she's gorgeous, sweet-natured, intelligent—"

"She's six weeks old! You have no idea how intelligent she is. And she was three weeks late," Casey grumbled. "She's going to have to improve her timing."

"Takes after her grandmother," Adam said, and dodged the swat Casey aimed at him. "Speaking of her, what time are Eloise and Sam due?"

Casey looked at her watch. "Right about now."

"Good, that gives us at least half an hour. Ever since they got married, Sam's been as hopeless as Eloise at getting anywhere on time."

"Half an hour for what? Oh!" Casey squealed as Adam swung her up into his arms and carried her along the hallway to their bedroom. He staggered slightly and she said, "I still weigh a ton from having your baby, don't I? Admit it."

"Never," he said through gritted teeth. He deposited her on the bed, then pulled off his T-shirt and lay down beside her, propped up on one elbow. With his free hand, he began to unbutton her shirt.

Casey felt the heat between them, so familiar yet still untamed. She tugged Adam's head down to hers.

"Are you sure you're ready for this?" he said, an inch from her lips. "Because if I kiss you now, there'll be no stopping me."

Thrilled at the thought, she brushed the briefest, teasing kiss across his mouth, so that he groaned when she pulled away. "The Adam Carmichael I married prided himself on always staying in control." She ran a tantalizing hand down his bare chest.

In a movement so swift it startled Casey, he straddled her. His strong hands pinned hers to the pillow and he covered her mouth with a kiss so hungry, so tender, so loving, that she seriously considered never leaving this bed again.

"In that case," he said, "I must apologize for the total loss of control you're about to experience."

With a sigh of satisfaction Casey gave herself up to his demanding caress. "Apology accepted," she murmured.

* * * * *

Set in darkness beyond the ordinary world.
Passionate tales of life and death.
With characters' lives ruled by laws the everyday
world can't begin to imagine.

n●cturne

It's time to discover the Raintree trilogy....

New York Times *bestselling author*
LINDA HOWARD
brings you the dramatic first book
RAINTREE: INFERNO

The Ansara Wizards are rising and the
Raintree clan must rejoin the battle against
their foes, testing their powers, relationships,
and forcing upon them lives they never
could have imagined before....

Turn the page for a sneak preview
of the captivating first book
in the Raintree trilogy,
RAINTREE: INFERNO
by LINDA HOWARD
On sale April 2.

Dante Raintree stood with his arms crossed as he watched the woman on the monitor. The image was in black and white to better show details; color distracted the brain. He focused on her hands, watching every move she made, but what struck him most was how uncommonly *still* she was. She didn't fidget or play with her chips, or look around at the other players. She peeked once at her down card, then didn't touch it again, signaling for another hit by tapping a fingernail on the table. Just because she didn't seem to be paying attention to the other players, though, didn't mean she was as unaware as she seemed.

"What's her name?" Dante asked.

"Lorna Clay," replied his chief of security, Al Rayburn.

"At first I thought she was counting, but she doesn't pay enough attention."

"She's paying attention, all right," Dante murmured. "You just don't see her doing it." A card counter had to remember every card played. Supposedly counting cards was impossible with the number of decks used by the casinos, but there were those rare individuals who could calculate the odds even with multiple decks.

"I thought that, too," said Al. "But look at this piece of tape coming up. Someone she knows comes up to her and speaks, she looks around and starts chatting, completely misses the play of the people to her left—and doesn't look around even when the deal comes back to her, just taps that finger. And damn if she didn't win. Again."

Dante watched the tape, rewound it, watched it again. Then he watched it a third time. There had to be something he was missing, because he couldn't pick out a single giveaway.

"If she's cheating," Al said with something like respect, "she's the best I've ever seen."

"What does your gut say?"

Al scratched the side of his jaw, considering. Finally, he said, "If she isn't cheating, she's the luckiest person walking. She wins. Week in, week out, she wins. Never a huge amount, but I ran the numbers and she's into us for about five grand a week. Hell, boss, on her way out of the casino she'll stop by a slot machine, feed a dollar in and walk away with at least fifty. It's never the same machine, either. I've had her watched, I've had her followed, I've even looked for the same faces in the casino every time she's in here, and I can't find a common denominator."

"Is she here now?"

"She came in about half an hour ago. She's playing blackjack, as usual."

"Bring her to my office," Dante said, making a swift decision. "Don't make a scene."

"Got it," said Al, turning on his heel and leaving the security center.

Dante left, too, going up to his office. His face was calm. Normally he would leave it to Al to deal with a cheater, but he was curious. How was she doing it? There were a lot of bad cheaters, a few good ones, and every so often one would come along who was the stuff of which legends were made: the cheater who didn't get caught, even when people were alert and the camera was on him—or, in this case, her.

It was possible to simply be lucky, as most people understood luck. Chance could turn a habitual loser into a big-time winner. Casinos, in fact, thrived on that hope. But luck itself wasn't habitual, and he knew that what passed for luck was often something else: cheating. And there was the other kind of luck, the kind he himself possessed, but it depended not on chance but on who and what he was. He knew it was an innate power and not Dame Fortune's erratic smile. Since power like his was rare, the odds made it likely the woman he'd been watching was merely a very clever cheat.

Her skill could provide her with a very good living, he thought, doing some swift calculations in his head. Five grand a week equaled $260,000 a year, and that was just from his casino. She probably hit them all, careful to keep the numbers relatively low so she stayed under the radar.

He wondered how long she'd been taking him, how long she'd been winning a little here, a little there, before Al noticed.

The curtains were open on the wall-to-wall window in his office, giving the impression, when one first opened the door, of stepping out onto a covered balcony. The glazed window faced west, so he could catch the sunsets. The sun was low now, the sky painted in purple and gold. At his home in the mountains, most of the windows faced east, affording him views of the sunrise. Something in him needed both the greeting and the goodbye of the sun. He'd always been drawn to sunlight, maybe because fire was his element to call, to control.

He checked his internal time: four minutes until sundown. Without checking the sunrise tables every day, he knew exactly when the sun would slide behind the mountains. He didn't own an alarm clock. He didn't need one. He was so acutely attuned to the sun's position that he had only to check within himself to know the time. As for waking at a particular time, he was one of those people who could tell himself to wake at a certain time, and he did. That talent had nothing to do with being Raintree, so he didn't have to hide it; a lot of perfectly ordinary people had the same ability.

He had other talents and abilities, however, that did require careful shielding. The long days of summer instilled in him an almost sexual high, when he could feel contained power buzzing just beneath his skin. He had to be doubly careful not to cause candles to leap into flame just by his presence, or to start wildfires with a glance in the dry-as-tinder brush. He loved Reno; he didn't want to burn it down. He just felt so damn *alive* with all the sunshine pouring down that he wanted to let the energy pour through him instead of holding it inside.

This must be how his brother Gideon felt while pulling lightning, all that hot power searing through his muscles, his veins. They had this in common, the connection with raw power. All the members of the far-flung Raintree clan had some power, some heightened ability, but only members of the royal family could channel and control the earth's natural energies.

Dante wasn't just of the royal family, he was the Dranir, the leader of the entire clan. "Dranir" was synonymous with king, but the position he held wasn't ceremonial, it was one of sheer power. He was the oldest son of the previous Dranir, but he would have been passed over for the position if he hadn't also inherited the power to hold it.

Behind him came Al's distinctive knock on the door. The outer office was empty, Dante's secretary having gone home hours before. "Come in," he called, not turning from his view of the sunset.

The door opened, and Al said, "Mr. Raintree, this is Lorna Clay."

Dante turned and looked at the woman, all his senses on alert. The first thing he noticed was the vibrant color of her hair, a rich, dark red that encompassed a multitude of shades from copper to burgundy. The warm amber light danced along the iridescent strands, and he felt a hard tug of sheer lust in his gut. Looking at her hair was almost like looking at fire, and he had the same reaction.

The second thing he noticed was that she was spitting mad.

nocturne™

IT'S TIME TO DISCOVER
THE RAINTREE TRILOGY...

There have always been those among us
who are more than human...

Don't miss the dramatic first book by
New York Times bestselling author

LINDA
HOWARD

RAINTREE:
Inferno

On sale May.

Raintree: Haunted by Linda Winstead Jones
Available June.

Raintree: Sanctuary by Beverly Barton
Available July.

REQUEST YOUR FREE BOOKS!
2 FREE NOVELS PLUS 2 *FREE GIFTS!*

HARLEQUIN®

Super Romance®

Exciting, emotional, unexpected!

YES! Please send me 2 FREE Harlequin Superromance® novels and my 2 FREE gifts. After receiving them, if I don't wish to receive any more books, I can return the shipping statement marked "cancel." If I don't cancel, I will receive 6 brand-new novels every month and be billed just $4.69 per book in the U.S., or $5.24 per book in Canada, plus 25¢ shipping and handling per book and applicable taxes, if any*. That's a savings of close to 15% off the cover price! I understand that accepting the 2 free books and gifts places me under no obligation to buy anything. I can always return a shipment and cancel at any time. Even if I never buy another book from Harlequin, the two free books and gifts are mine to keep forever.   135 HDN EEX7 336 HDN EEYK

Name	(PLEASE PRINT)

Address	Apt.

City	State/Prov.	Zip/Postal Code

Signature (if under 18, a parent or guardian must sign)

Mail to the **Harlequin Reader Service**®:
IN U.S.A.: P.O. Box 1867, Buffalo, NY 14240-1867
IN CANADA: P.O. Box 609, Fort Erie, Ontario L2A 5X3

Not valid to current Harlequin Superromance subscribers.

Want to try two free books from another line?
Call 1-800-873-8635 or visit www.morefreebooks.com.

* Terms and prices subject to change without notice. NY residents add applicable sales tax. Canadian residents will be charged applicable provincial taxes and GST. This offer is limited to one order per household. All orders subject to approval. Credit or debit balances in a customer's account(s) may be offset by any other outstanding balance owed by or to the customer. Please allow 4 to 6 weeks for delivery.

Your Privacy: Harlequin is committed to protecting your privacy. Our Privacy Policy is available online at www.eHarlequin.com or upon request from the Reader Service. From time to time we make our lists of customers available to reputable firms who may have a product or service of interest to you. If you would prefer we not share your name and address, please check here. ☐

HSR07